THE
TOMORROW
CONNECTION

T. Ernesto Bethancourt

THE
TOMORROW
CONNECTION

Holiday House / New York

Library of Congress Cataloging in Publication Data

Bethancourt, T. Ernesto.
The tomorrow connection.

Summary: Two musicians, finding themselves stranded in
1906, enlist Harry Houdini to help them find a gate to
the future and travel across the country on the vaudeville
circuit, to arrive in San Francisco just in time for
the great earthquake.
[1. Space and time—Fiction. 2. United States—Social
life and customs—1865–1918—Fiction. 3. San Francisco
(Calif.)—Earthquake, 1906—Fiction. 4. Houdini, Harry,
1874–1926—Fiction] I. Title.
PZ7.B46627To   1984   [Fic]   84-47836
ISBN 0-8234-0543-5

For all magicians, amateur and professional, who have delighted millions since time began, and for MARGERY CUYLER, who has worked her own brand of magic with the author's manuscripts for ten years.

Contents

Foreword

As in any novel with a historical setting, I have tried as best I could to maintain absolute accuracy as to location, customs, and speech. There have been some changes made, dictated by dramatic necessity. Some social attitudes and slur terms for minorities have been retained to convey the flavor of the period, but for those offended by such words, I must point out that they were the common usage of the day and accepted as such by all, save to whom they were applied.

For example, "coon acts" in vaudeville were called that, and no amount of sanding and varnishing can impart a sheen to this regrettable piece of show business history. By true count, according to my research, in 1907 there were 270 blacks rated as principals in the theater, and an estimated 1,400 in show business all together. The black vaudeville acts named in this book are real. The character of Manfred the Great is fictional.

For those interested in the life of the Great Houdini, as well as in the fascinating world that was vaudeville, there is a partial bibliography at the end of the book.

T. E. Bethancourt

Alta Loma, California
1983

THE
TOMORROW
CONNECTION

1

Turn Back the Hands of Time

A bright light shone into my eyes. A voice from behind the light said, "Hold it right there, you two. In case you can't see it, I got a ten-gauge shotgun here. If either one of you moves, I can cut you both in half!"

I groaned inwardly and raised my hands over my head. My pal, Matty Owen, did the same. Geez, I thought, I hope this guy isn't trigger happy. If he shoots Matty and me, I don't know what'll happen. On account of neither one of us is due to be born for another forty-six years, that'll be 1958.

If all of this sounds weird, that's because it is. You see, Matty and I are time travelers. Not like the kind you see on TV or in movies. I wish it were that simple to go bouncing around in time... having lunch with Julius Caesar, dinner with George Washington, and stuff like that. Traveling in time is a very complicated business. Like the situation Matty and I found ourselves in right then.

We were in the year 1912. We didn't pick the year. But we had to get away from the year we'd been visiting, 1942. We're both originally from the year 1976. In '76, I was,

3

and I guess I still am, a high school senior in a small town on Long Island, New York. The name of the town is Branford. In fact, we were still in Branford, but sixty-four years earlier in history.

In spite of what you may have seen or read in science fiction novels, when you travel in time, you go back or forward to exactly the same place you left. Only the time changes, not the location. If you want to go someplace while in the time period, you have to travel in the same way as anyone else. You walk or drive or fly. In our case, in 1912, there were no airplanes carrying passengers, and very few cars.

"All right, now," the voice from behind the light said to us, "come closer. Into the light."

Matty and I obliged. Sure enough, the owner of the voice and the lantern was aiming a shotgun at us. It looked more like a cannon. I could also see the man holding the gun. He was in his mid-fifties, I'd say. Real old, anyhow. He was wearing dark trousers, a white shirt with no tie, an open vest, and a dark felt hat. Pinned to his vest was a shiny six-pointed metal star. The guy was some kind of lawman. He came around behind Matty and me and said, "March. Straight ahead to the cemetery gate. Don't try to run. You can't outrun a ten-gauge. My Model-T is right outside the gate. You two lean on it, over the hood...."

We did as we were told. When we got to the car, I couldn't help but look it over, the way Matty was doing. Back in our own time, we're both old car freaks. We'd seen restored Model-Ts, but never a brand-new one. I hated to lean on it and make fingerprints on the hood.

It was an open touring model, and it didn't bother this cop, or whatever he was, to set the lantern down on its hood. I heard him fumbling around in the back seat of the car, but I didn't look his way. No point in getting shot just for curiosity's sake.

The guy patted us down for concealed weapons in a professional manner, then took out two pairs of handcuffs. In a short time, we were both handcuffed to the folding top of the Ford, in the back seat.

The man with the badge adjusted the spark and throttle controls of the car, which are on the steering column on Model-Ts, then went around in front, and twisted the crank. There may have been self-starters on some cars in 1912, but there weren't on Fords. The engine caught immediately, and the man got behind the wheel. We chugged off toward Branford at a brisk fifteen miles per hour. I know the town is two miles from the cemetery we were in, and I figured the trip would take only a few minutes.

Matty leaned over and whispered to me: "What *is* this? Do they arrest you for being in a cemetery after dark in 1912?"

"How should I know?" I whispered back. "We have to wait and see what this is all about. In the meantime, why don't you start thinking up some explanation...who we are, what we're doing here and all?"

"That's a tall order, my man," Matty said, "but I'll try."

As we jounced along the unpaved road, I thought back on why we were there. The real reasons. Why Richie Gilroy and Matty Owen, both age eighteen, both jazz musicians and nostalgia buffs, had been arrested in a deserted graveyard in the year A.D. 1912. If I told the man driving the car the truth, we wouldn't be put in jail. We'd be put in an insane asylum. Sometimes I have trouble believing the truth myself.

Nineteen seventy-six was not a very good year for either Matty or me. He was in trouble at home, with his dad. Matty's mom had died a few years before, and his older sister was running the household. She and Matty didn't get on at all. And whenever there was a hassle, Matty's dad would take the sister's side.

My home life, if you could call it that, was even worse. My folks have been divorced for years. My dad, Harry, went middle-aged crazy and was dating girls not much older than me. Mom took the breakup real hard. She began drinking so heavy that I was really the head of the house, and taking care of her. I kept the bank balance, cashed the checks that Harry sent, and paid the bills. I had to. If Mom got hold of one of Harry's support checks, she'd drink it up in a few days. So, if Matty had a bum home life, I didn't have one at all.

It was about then that I stumbled on the gate to the past. I mean, literally. Matty and I were part of this wimpy Bicentennial parade the Junior Chamber of Commerce in Branford got together. They used our high school band, and had us dressed in these tacky Revolutionary War get-ups. The parade started in the middle of Branford and ended up at the cemetery, which does have gravestones dating back to the 1700s. The whole thing was to commemorate the Battle of Branford. What the Jaycees didn't mention was that the British *won* that battle. Branford's always been a loser town.

Matty marched with me. He plays in the marching band, too. Talk about being an operator. When the band got to the graveyard, hot and thirsty, all the other guys had to look forward to was a long walk back. But for just him and

me, Matty had hidden a six-pack of soda in a cooler, behind
a gravestone in a seldom-used part of the cemetery. Like
I say, he thinks ahead. I remember that we even commented on the funny name of the man buried under the
stone: Abner Pew. His epitaph read:

HERE LIE THE REMAINS OF
ABNER PEW, FREEMAN,
DIED JUNE 16, 1778.
HIS VALOUR IN SAVING THE LIFE
OF NATHANIEL BRANFORD
WON FOR HIM HIS FREEDOM.
MAY THE FREEDOM BORN OF BATTLE
ENDURE LONGER THAN THIS STONE.
R.I.P.

We congratulated ourselves on the stash, and while I
was paying Matty a few dollars I owed him, I accidentally
left my wallet on top of the gravestone. It wasn't until I
got home that I realized I must have left it there. I went
back on my bike in the dark to retrieve it. But when I did,
I walked right into the past...Revolutionary War times,
to be exact.

It seems that there are places in the world where time
forms a warp, or a snarl. If you know the routine and
movements, you can step from the present right into the
past. Or even the future, depending on what kind of gate
you use. In this case, the Branford Gate, it's to the past.

To keep a lot of people from stumbling through the
gates, like I did, there are people watching them. They're
called gatekeepers, and Abner Pew was one of them. Yes,
Pew is still alive, or maybe what I saw in the graveyard was

a ghost. I still don't know. But Abner Pew looked solid enough to me. The reason he let me pass through was funny.

I was dressed like a Revolutionary War soldier. And purely by accident, I did the little combination of steps at the gravestone that led him to believe I was a regular time traveler. He let me through, although I didn't see him at the time.

But I didn't know I'd gone back in time to the 1700s. I thought I was still in 1976 Branford. Until I walked into town and found everything different. I thought I was losing my marbles. I retraced my steps to the graveyard, not knowing it was the thing to do, and I popped right back into 1976. Just dumb luck that I didn't get stranded in Revolutionary War times. I didn't even see Abner Pew until later, when I went back to the graveyard with Matty the next night. I wanted Matty to go with me to act as a witness to the fact that weird things were going down in the Branford cemetery.

Matty saw Abner, too. That's when Pew told us his life story, and how he came to be gatekeeper. That's also when I saw a chance to get out of the rotten life I was leading. I pitched the idea to Matty. We were both nostalgia buffs. What could be neater than going back to the 1940s, when the big bands were playing and they had all those swift old cars?

Matty was lukewarm about the idea. He pointed out what Pew had told us. If we stayed more than an hour in the past, we were stuck there. The only way back to our own time would be by a future gate. And Pew didn't know where the future gates were; just his own gate. It sounded too risky to Matty. But things took a nasty turn for both of us about then.

Matty's eighteenth birthday did it. We were celebrating the fact that in 1976, you could drink legally in New York at eighteen. We had more than a few beers, and when we got back to Matty's house, he parked the Chevy he'd restored on the front lawn. Matty's dad wanted to ground him, but Matty argued that he was now an adult. Matty's dad countered by ordering him out of the house if he was so grown up. He also threatened to cut off paying Matty's tuition to the Juilliard School of Music. Matty had passed the entrance exam just a few weeks earlier. Now he was broke, with no place to live. Sure, he could have apologized to his dad, but he was being stubborn.

For me, it was even worse. I flunked the Juilliard exam. All I had to look forward to was pouring my mother into bed at night and kicking out the occasional visitor I'd find sleeping one off in my bed. When I raised the issue of going back in time to Matty again, he agreed.

We studied up on the 1940s, so we wouldn't make any bad mistakes when we got there. We got clothes that would pass for forties stuff. The big problem was money. Try passing a ten-dollar bill in 1942, when the date on it reads: *Series E, 1976.* Luckily, I had a coin collection, mostly silver dollars, made before the 1940s. All dressed up, Matty and I went to see Abner Pew.

I'm not proud of what we did. We tricked Pew. We brought a bottle of 151-proof rum with us. That stuff's dynamite. Pew had told us he hadn't had a drink in nearly two hundred years. The way he went at the jug, I believed him. When he was pretty well stoned, we slipped through the gate to the past. But before we did, I asked the fuzzy-minded Pew about how we could find a future gate.

He gave me a big, old-fashioned iron key that he kept on his belt. Pew said that when we got close to a future gate, the key would glow in the dark and grow warm to the touch. As to where the gate could be found, all he said was, "Where the compass needle spins and the horizon changes places with the sea..." Then he passed out, and we slipped into the past.

And into such trouble as anyone ever saw. We were nearly killed by Nazi saboteurs who firebombed the French Liner *Normandie* in New York harbor in 1942. While we were trying to stop them, the cops showed up. They thought *we* were the saboteurs. After a wild car chase in a "borrowed" Cord supercharged convertible, we got to Branford and the gate to the past just a few seconds ahead of the cops.

We ducked inside the gate and told Abner to send us anywhere, as long as it wasn't 1942. So he sent us to 1912. No sooner were we out of the gate when this guy with the shotgun and lantern showed up. And here we were, headed for Branford, in a brand-new 1912 Model-T. With handcuffs on!

I leaned over to Matty and whispered, "Any ideas yet?" He shook his head no. But I wasn't all that worried. I have a lot of faith in Matty. If there's an angel, he can find it. I sometimes think he overcomplicates things, just for the fun of the scheming he gets to do. And rap? Matty Owen could charm a cobra into being his necktie. If Matty ever wore ties, that is.

Not that his quick mind did us all that good in 1942. People wouldn't give him a chance to run his scams. That's on account of Matty being black. Back in 1942, in the heart of "liberal" New York City, most hotels and restaurants wouldn't let blacks in the door. Not the front door, anyhow. If they were kitchen help or janitors, that was different. But blacks couldn't handle food in public. All the waiters and even the bellhops were white.

This came as quite a shock to Matty. See, he's been raised in a well-to-do family. His dad owns an electronics firm that sells a lot of gadgets to the Brookhaven Labs on Long Island. Matty grew up with only the best. He had his own car when he was sixteen.

Which isn't to say that Matty's a spoiled rich kid. He's a real person, and the best friend I've ever had. We were tight all through junior high and high school. We did have a little trouble when we started double-dating. Even in 1976, you didn't cross racial lines that easy.

But in 1942, Matty was miserable, and you can't blame him. The first time he ran into race prejudice, he wanted to head right back to 1976. Not that it's so great today. But by then, we were stuck in the past. Unless we could find one of the future gates Abner Pew had spoken of.

The Model-T was rolling into downtown Branford. By downtown, I mean there were streetlights and sidewalks. Houses closer together. Even in 1976, Branford wasn't big. But in 1912, with a good tailwind, you could probably spit from one end of unpaved Main Street to the other. The guy with the tin star turned off Main and down Oak.

"Any ideas yet?" I asked Matty.

"Don't rush me," he said impatiently. "I can't figure out anything until I know why this jerk up there arrested us. If it's only trespassing in the cemetery, we can talk our way out...say we got lost."

"And if it isn't for trespassing?"

"I don't know. But what else could it be? We haven't been in 1912 long enough to do anything."

The guy with the badge stopped the car in front of a white frame house on Oak Street. I recognized it. It's still standing in my time. In another sixty-four years, it would be the Branford Historical Society and Museum, run by my old history teacher, Mrs. Krendler. But just now, it was a private house. There was a sign on the lawn. It read: *J. R. Minton, Justice of the Peace.*

The sheriff, or whatever he was, killed the Ford's motor and unchained us from the car. He then handcuffed us together, while keeping his shotgun cradled in the crook of his right arm.

"Out of the car, and get up on the porch," he commanded. We did what he said, and when we got to the front door of the house, we stood aside while he rang the doorbell. In a few minutes, the curtains on the half-glass door parted, and the face of a man about forty peeked out. Then he opened the door wide.

He was dressed in dark trousers, a white shirt with no collar, and so help me, a smoking jacket. It was blue velvet, with black satin lapels. He had slippers on his feet with Indian heads embroidered on them.

"Hello, Lem," the man said. "What have you got here?"

"Found 'em in the cemetery, yerhonor," Lem said.

"Grave robbers, eh?"

"Not that I saw, Judge Minton," Lem replied. "But they fit the descriptions of them two escaped convicts the whole county's been looking fer. The ones that busted out of the Raymond Street Jail in Brooklyn last week. Didn't you see the reports we got yesterday? Came in on the six-fifteen train."

"To tell the truth, Lem, I haven't," the man said. "I've been too busy with this fuss about women voting. That parade they held on Sunday, when you had to arrest Miss Frances."

"Served her right, too," Lem grumbled. "A woman teaching school oughta know her place...not go marching around, stirring up things. It sets a bad example for the kids she teaches."

"Well, come in, come in," the judge said. "Let's have a look at what you've caught."

"Move," Lem said, prodding me in the back with his shotgun. Matty and I went into the house, then turned to the left as the judge pointed to a set of sliding doors, which he rolled open. The room was set up as part living room, part courtroom. It was dimly lit by gaslights, turned down low. Funny, I'd expected electric lights. I knew they were already invented. But like I said, Branford's always been backward.

We stood in the middle of the room while Minton walked around us, inspecting us like we were some new animal in a biology class.

"They fit the descriptions, all right, yerhonor," Lem said, "About twenty years old. One white, one nigger. Both tall."

I saw Matty's reaction to the word. Like he'd been slapped in the face. He controlled himself, though.

"You, boy," the judge said to me. "What's your name?"

"Richard Gilroy, sir," I said.

"And where are you from, Richard?"

That was a sticky question. I couldn't say I was from

Branford. We were *in* Branford. And there wasn't a soul there who would know me, or even my family. We moved to Branford from Manhattan when I was eight years old. Even if I told the truth and said I was from Branford, the judge would know I was "lying."

"Well, speak up, Richard," the judge said. "Where are you from? And what were you doing in the cemetery at eight o'clock at night?" He turned to Lem and asked, "Come to think of it, Lem, what were *you* doing there?"

"Got some reports of stolen chickens from the Smith farm. Figured it might be the two convicts, hiding out and stealing food. I was right, too."

"We were lost, your honor, and we didn't steal any chickens," Matty said.

Judge Minton turned to Matty and frowned. "Speak when you're spoken to, boy," he said abruptly and turned his attention back to me. Just like that. He'd completely dismissed Matty as someone to talk to. That was too bad. I'd counted on Matty to come up with some alibi. But it was 1942 all over again. Blacks weren't supposed to have anything to say.

"We're from New York City," I blurted out.

"Liar!" Lem snapped. "You're from the Brooklyn jail, and you broke out last week! That nigger there killed a white man. I'd just as soon shoot both of you right now. Or even better, I got a good rope out in the car. I can have 'em both swinging from a tree, yerhonor," he added to Judge Minton. "Just say the word. No one'll know but us."

2

Let Me Go, Brother

"Don't be foolish, Lem," Judge Minton said. "If these men are the two convicts—and we don't know they are for sure—we have to turn them over to the Brooklyn authorities. Do you have the wanted notice?"

"Out in the car, yerhonor."

"Then go get it," Minton said. "If they're the wanted men, we'll soon find out."

Lem left, and the judge looked me over again. "What is your relationship to this colored boy?" he asked.

"He's my friend, your honor," I said.

"You should pick your friends more carefully," he replied.

"Maybe we all should," I said, nodding toward outside, where Lem had gone to get the wanted notice. I knew it was a mistake to mouth off at a judge, but I'd had enough cheap shots aimed at my pal Matty.

"Meaning *what?*" the judge asked in a nasty tone.

I glanced over at Matty. He gave me a look that plainly said, *Cool it.* I recovered fast and said to Judge Minton, "I mean, we should all be careful of the company we keep, sir. So we don't fall in with a bad crowd, like you said."

"Quite true," the judge answered. He glanced at my clothes. "I'd say you haven't been traveling in the best of circles for some time, young man. You could do with a bath and a shave, you know. However, you seem to be a polite and well-spoken young fellow."

What he said was true. Not about the way I talk. My clothes. Matty and I had dropped into 1912 after a wild car chase and scrambling around in a dark graveyard. We were both a mess.

"As I said, your honor," I went on, "we're looking for work. We haven't had a chance to bathe or shave. We haven't eaten in so long, I can't remember when it was...."

"Hmmm," Minton said. "Well, you'll find very few hand-outs in Branford. We don't have a regular jail, either. But I'll have the hired girl make up something for you before we lock you up."

That didn't sound encouraging at all. Locked up for what? We weren't the guys they were looking for. But evidently, they weren't taking any chances. So much for civil rights in Branford, I thought. It must have hit Matty the same way. He said to the judge, "On what charges are you going to lock us up? We're entitled to know. It's in the Constitution."

"What would you know of the Constitution, boy?" he rapped.

"No citizen can be deprived of life, liberty, or property without due process of Law," Matty came back. "It's in the Bill of Rights...one of the amendments."

Minton's eyes grew wide and his mouth dropped open. He was astonished that Matty could know such things. He gave me a stern look and said, "You've been teaching your friend, Richard," he accused. "Teaching him things he'd be better off not knowing." He frowned. "Bad enough they're learning to read and write. Nothing stirs up the coloreds like education. A little knowledge can be a dangerous thing."

Matty was about to say something when Lem came back in. He had a piece of paper in his hand. "Got the wanted notice right here, yerhonor," he said. He handed the printed form to the judge, who took a pair of round, steel-rimmed eyeglasses from his vest pocket. As he read it, he kept glancing up at Matty and me, comparing us with the description on the form.

"Lift up your trouser legs, both of you," he said suddenly. We did like he said. He bent down and examined our shoes. At least that's what I thought he was doing. He snorted and stood up. "Now roll up your shirtsleeves," he said. Puzzled, we obeyed.

Minton walked over to the sheriff and put a hand on the bigger man's shoulder. "It's not them," he said flatly.

"How do you know that, yerhonor?" Lem asked.

"Look at their ankles and wrists, man," the judge responded. "This poster says that the two men who escaped from Brooklyn were recalcitrants...."

"What's that yerhonor?"

"Troublemakers, Lem. Troublemakers," the judge said, with a hint of a smile. "The report also says that for trying to break out last year, they were both put in irons for six months. As soon as they were let out of the irons, they tried to escape again. This time, they succeeded."

"All right, they don't have cuffs or leg irons on them. They could have sawed them off somehow. Besides, you said they was let out of irons. That's why you didn't see none when you checked their legs and wrists."

The judge sighed deeply. "Lem, use your horse sense. A man who's been in leg and wrist irons for half a year would have scars, or at least marks where the irons had been. Neither of these boys has a mark on him. On top of that, the report says that the white man is twenty-five years old. This boy isn't twenty, I'm sure. And the colored escapee is described as having a scar on his left cheek. This boy is unmarked. No, Lem. They're not the men listed in this report."

"Then who are they?"

"Has it ever occurred to you that they might be telling the truth? That they are drifters, looking for work?"

"Then what was they doing in the graveyard?"

"Like they said: they were lost. Or looking for a free place to sleep. It doesn't matter, really. Just lock them up in the shed, Lem."

"What for?" I burst out.

"Vagrancy," said the judge. "We don't take kindly to tramps in Branford. My judgment is that you serve thirty days' hard labor. There is a lot of work for idle hands in Branford."

"What kind of justice is this?" I demanded. "We aren't the escaped convicts. Why don't you just let us go? We'll be on our way in the morning. We'll go back to New York."

"Oh, you'll stay in Branford, all right," the judge said with an oily smile. "We're paving downtown Main Street. With good Belgian granite blocks. They weigh about twenty pounds apiece. The masons lay the blocks, but someone carries them to the stonesetters...you two. A strapping boy like that one over there could carry a hundred pounds at a time, easily."

"Is this America?" Matty demanded. "No trial, no nothing. Just some two-bit justice of the peace playing God?"

"Your sentence is now ninety days of hard labor, nigger," the judge said. "And in case you're wondering what the charge is, it's contempt of court! Lock them up, Lem."

Lem led us outside to the backyard of the frame house. There was a barn, a stable, and a woodshed. He swung open the door to the shed and motioned us to go inside. I noticed that the woodshed door was held closed by a hasp and eye catch, with a padlock. It might be easy to kick down later. But even though he knew we weren't escapees, Lem didn't take the cuffs off us. He just recuffed us separately, our hands in front of us.

"Make yerselves comfortable, boys," he said. "Big day for you tomorrow. Lotta work to do."

"What about the food the judge promised us?" I asked.

"You'll get it," Lem replied. "The hired girl is probably putting it together right now." He waved an arm toward the house. "There's a light on in the kitchen. In the meantime, don't start thinking of breaking out. You won't get far. I got the best tracking dogs in Branford."

He swung the shed door closed. It was pitch-dark inside, except for the few rays of light that came through the unsealed boards of the woodshed. Once we heard Lem's heavy footsteps receding, Matty turned to me and said, "Richie, we have to get out of here. Before daybreak, too. If we can make it back to the cemetery, we'll be able to get out of 1912."

"And go where?" I asked. "Back further into the past?

Every time we make one of these jumps, we get into trouble. To make it worse, each time we go further back, we know less and less about the year we land in."

"Guess you're right, pal. Maybe we should have paid more attention to Mrs. Krendler in history class. But it's a little late in the game to be thinking of that, isn't it?"

I didn't answer. We both fell silent for a time. I figured that Matty was hatching some plot, and I didn't want to disturb his thoughts. I was wracking my brain, too. Just then, there was a rattling noise, and the woodshed door swung open. I found myself face to face with a black woman in her sixties. She was holding a lantern in one hand and a plate of sandwiches in the other. In the crook of her elbow, she had a tin pail with its handle over her arm.

"Move away from the door, or you don't get nothing to eat," she commanded. We moved back and she set down the plate and can, never taking her eyes off us. I saw then that the can held milk.

"Nothing fancy," the woman said, "just leftover ham sandwiches. But the milk is fresh enough." She took a few steps backward and said, "All right. Help yourselfs."

We didn't need an engraved invitation. Matty and I swooped down on the sandwiches. The woman kept watching us as we ate. Maybe she was waiting for the empty plate and milk can. At first, being watched while I ate didn't matter. But once we were down to just one sandwich, her stern, steady stare made me edgy.

"You. Colored boy," she said suddenly to Matty. "What's your name?"

"Owen...Matthew Owen, ma'am," Matty said around a mouthful of ham sandwich.

"You're gonna get yourself in a whole lot of trouble, you know that?" she said. "Talking that way to Judge Minton. Don't you have any sense at all, boy?"

"Well, it isn't legal, you know...what he did to us," Matty said.

"Seems you got some education, Matthew," the woman said, "but you don't have the common sense God gave a cockroach. First off, it doesn't matter what white folks do, legal or no. They're the white folks, and they do it. You're colored, and the rules ain't for you."

"That's not so," Matty said hotly. "The laws are for all people, black or white. That's what the Constitution is all about. If you only stand up to these people..."

"You get knocked right on your black behind," the woman broke in. She snorted in disgust. "You smart hotheads with all your book learning. You forget one thing: there's two kinds of law in this country. One is for white folks and the other is for coloreds. And don't you ever think it's not so. No, don't open your educated mouth to me, Matthew Owen. I'm still talking. Wasn't you taught to respect your elders?

"Now, tomorrow, you're going to be doing road work for Sheriff Albertson. I'm gonna give you a hint, Matthew. Do your work and keep your mouth shut. Don't go talking about laws and what white folks are supposed to do. That man, Albertson, is mean right down to his shoe leather. Ain't a thing he likes more than breaking the head of some colored boy who gets sassy with him."

"If we're still here tomorrow morning, I'll keep it in mind, lady," Matty said.

The woman's face fell. "Don't go thinking about running

away, Matthew," she cautioned. "Sheriff Albertson's got a whole pack of dogs. And he likes to use that shotgun of his, too. He killed a man once, they say."

"We'll be careful, lady," I said.

"My name's Lily," the woman said, looking at me for what seemed like the first time. "I'm the hired girl and cook here. Have been for ten years, since my mister died. You don't have to call me *lady*. Just Lily."

"You do have a last name, don't you?" I asked.

"Of course I do," she said quickly. "My family name is Gilchrist. You think I was born a slave, with no family name? Our family is from right here, on Long Island. There been Gilchrists here since the 1700s. Freemen, every last one. We've never been slaves. The idea! No family name! You think we're like some of that trash comes up from the South?"

"Sorry, Mrs. Gilchrist," I said hurriedly, "I didn't mean any offense."

"I told you. My name's Lily...." She gave me another once-over with her piercing dark eyes. "You know," she said, "you are the strangest pair I ever did see. Don't either one of you know nothing about anything in this world? Where are you from? Where did you grow up? Who's your folks?"

"It's a long story, Mrs. Gilchrist," Matty said. "We grew up in another country."

I noticed that when Matty called the woman Mrs. Gilchrist, she didn't correct him. I decided that there were probably rules: Matty, being black, could call her Mrs. Gilchrist, but me being white, I was supposed to call her Lily. One thing was for sure. When Matty said he and I grew up in another country, he was right. For black people, the U.S.A. in 1976 was a completely different land from the U.S.A. in 1912. When Matty said "another country," though, her face lit up.

"You from Europe?" she asked, raising her eyebrows. "I heard say from the pastor at my church that things is different in Europe...like, say, in France. Reverend Michaels, he's been all over the world."

"Uh...yeah," Matty lied. "We're from France."

"You speak good enough English," Lily Gilchrist said suspiciously.

"Oh, our families are American," Matty said lying some more, "but Richie and I grew up together. We went to the same schools."

"They let you do that in France?" she asked, her eyes wide. She sighed. "I surely would like to see France someday," she said.

"Someday, it'll be like that in this country," Matty told her. "Someday, you'll see kids, black and white, attending the same schools, living in the same part of town. Blacks will go to colleges and universities...."

"They already doing that," Lily Gilchrist replied. "We got our own colleges. Tuskegee...Dr. Booker T. Washington's school for coloreds."

"No, Mrs. Gilchrist," Matty said. "I mean blacks going to a university like Yale or Harvard or Columbia...side by side with white students."

Mrs. Gilchrist exhaled heavily and picked up the now-empty plate and milk can. "You sure can talk, Matthew," she said, "but you're a dreamer. Frederick Douglass used to talk that way. I heard him once. My father took me all the way into New York City to hear him. That was a long, long time ago. And I ain't seen a thing changed, for all the talking. You better get your rest. Tomorrow, you're gonna be working your heart out on Main Street."

"You be sure to lock the shed door carefully, Mrs. Gilchrist," Matty said. "I don't want you to get in any trouble on our account."

"I told you, don't even *think* of running away!"

"But we have a place to go, ma'am," Matty insisted. "We could get back to France, if we can get out of this shed tonight. It's just that if we kick the door down, it'd make noise and wake the whole house. But if somebody forgot to padlock the shed…"

"Then you'd sneak out," she said scornfully. "Two boys on the run. In chains at that. How far do you think you'd get? As it is, the whole blessed county is out hunting those two convicts!"

"You heard every word that went on in the house, didn't you?" I asked. "You know we aren't those two guys. Funny, I didn't see you inside the house."

"I hear what I want to hear," she said with a smile. "And folks don't pay attention to a simple colored girl like me."

"You're far from simple," Matty said, walking toward her, "and you're no girl. You are a great lady, Lily Gilchrist." As he said it, Matty took her free hand in both of his chained ones. Then, just like some dude in a movie, he kissed her hand. "I am honored to have met you, ma'am," he said.

She pushed him aside roughly and muttered, "Fancified jackass." But she gave us both a smile that warmed the slight chill of the May night. She swung the door of the shed closed, and I heard her rattle the hasp. But there was one thing I didn't hear. Something I had heard when Albertson had shut us in. I didn't hear the padlock being snapped! We sat in the darkness for about five minutes, then I said to Matty, "She didn't spring the lock."

"I know," he said. "I didn't think she would."

"You're outrageous, you know that?" I said. "Lying to that nice lady that way. And you know she's gonna get in trouble for this, don't you?"

"That is one smart lady, Richie," Matty told me. "I'm willing to bet that when they find us gone tomorrow, and ask her, she's gonna put on a dumb act. They'll blame it on her being naturally stupid, like they think all blacks are. They'll chew her out, and that'll be the end of it."

"I hope you're right."

"So do I."

3

New York, New York

We eased out of the woodshed and into the yard. The door creaked a little, but not enough to wake anyone. The full moon was a great help. Otherwise we would have been falling all over ourselves in the dark. Something on a bush, right near the shed, caught my eye.

"Matty," I whispered, "what's that, over there?"

"Where? Where?" he whispered through his teeth, all panicky.

"Over there, in the bushes. That piece of white cloth."

"Don't *do* that," he said. "I thought you saw someone coming."

Matty went over and picked up the cloth, then came back to where I was. He opened up a square of muslin, tied shut like a little purse. He turned in the full moonlight and examined it.

"Well, I'll be..." he whispered.

"What is it?" I hissed.

"Look at this," Matty said. "It's a homemade handkerchief. I know because my grandmother used to make them, when I was a boy. I'd almost forgotten. Grandma used to take bedsheets that wore out and cut them into little squares. Then she'd sew a hem on them to make little handker-chiefs. She'd been doing it since she was a little girl. Learned it from *her* mother. When you're poor, nothing goes to waste."

"Swell," I said. "We're trying to escape from here, and you stand around talking about handkerchiefs. Are you nuts?"

"But look what's inside it, Richie," Matty said softly.

It was a fifty-cent piece. Bless Mrs. Gilchrist. She knew we were broke. Not only did she leave the shed door open, she left us some getaway money! I knew from 1942 that a half dollar was a lot of money back then. In 1906, it was probably worth even more. Who knows how long it had taken that nice lady to save it?

"You aren't gonna take it, are you?" I asked Matty.

"We have to," he replied. "If we leave it here, the sher-iff's men will spot it tomorrow. They'll know then how we got away."

"Okay, okay," I whispered impatiently, "now can we get out of here?"

We made our way out Main Street, avoiding the small circles of light cast by the old-fashioned streetlights. In a half-hour's time, we were standing in front of the grave-stone of Abner Pew.

"Pew!" I called out. "It's us. Matty Owen and Richie Gilroy. Abner! Where are you?"

"Do not cry out, young squire," rumbled a deep, bass voice from behind us. "I be not deef, y'know."

We spun around. There, standing in the moonlight be-hind us, was the biggest black man you'll ever see outside of the NBA. Abner Pew is easily six foot five and I'd say about three hundred pounds. And not an ounce of fat on him, either.

He was dressed straight out of a history book illustration for 1776: three-cornered hat, a big brass-buttoned coat, white shirt with a lace collar, riding pants with knee-high boots. He had a pair of flintlock pistols tucked into his wide belt, which also supported a nasty-looking saber. Pew looked at our handcuffs and chuckled: a sound like a fire engine starting up.

"I see ye have been enjoying the hospitality of the local townspeople," he said.

"A misunderstanding, Abner," Matty said. "They thought we were a couple of escaped convicts. We got away, though." He held up his manacled wrists. "Can you do anything about these?" he asked.

Pew didn't reply. He took both of Matty's hands in one of his massive paws and held them up in the moonlight. He then laughed outright.

"It be a marvel to me," he said, "that with all the new ways men devise to kill each other, they use the same old ways to keep each other in chains."

He reached down to the big key ring that hung from his belt. With unbelievable delicacy for the size of his hands, he selected a small, flat piece of steel. Not a key at all, really. He inserted the piece of metal into the lock of one of Matty's cuffs and gave a twist. With a click, the manacle flew open. In a few more seconds, he'd freed the both of us. Matty and I stood there, rubbing our wrists.

"Neat trick, Abner," I said appreciatively.

"Trick? A stratagem?" Abner Pew went on to say scornfully, "Nay, young squire. 'Tis Science. A lock is a simple mechanism. One need only know a tot of how they are constructed to open any lock made." He smiled, displaying surprisingly small teeth. "But what brings ye here?" he asked. "I mean, save to be unfettered by me?"

He looked at the handcuffs with distaste and, with a sudden motion, threw them easily fifty yards away. I heard a faint clink as they landed. "I have no great love for fetters, having spent some of my young life wearing them," he explained. "But ye have not answered my query. What seek ye from the keeper of the gate to the past?"

"We have to get out of 1912, Abner," Matty said. "In a few hours, there'll be a man with a pack of dogs and a gun after us."

"Ye have not slain a man, have ye?" Abner asked urgently, his smile fading, "for if ye have, there is little I may do to help thee. Stumbling about in time, destroying lives, ye may tear the very fabric of time itself. Ye might even wreak havoc upon the future!"

"No, no. Nothing like that, Abner," Matty said quickly. "They arrested us as vagrants. They were going to make us work, paving a road for the next three months."

"Be ye both so averse to honest labor that ye must flee in the face of it?" Abner asked.

"Not when they don't pay you and keep you in chains," Matty replied.

"Understandable," Pew rumbled. Then he spread his hands apart, waist-high. "But what would ye have me do? Send thee further back in time?"

"You got it, Abner," I said.

"Very well, young squire," he said. "Have ye a choice as to what year?"

"No," Matty said, "so long as it isn't 1912."

"We can't go too far back," I put in. "We're having enough trouble knowing how to act as it is."

"That's right," Matty said. "And it should be some time period where we can get work. I mean, besides carrying paving blocks. We don't want a year where there's a war going on, either."

"Ye ask a great deal, young squire," Pew said. "It be the most difficult thing to find a year when men do not war on each other."

"Well, at least where we can get work," Matty said. "Once we get some coins together, we'll be able to travel and find the future gate."

"There is merit in what ye say, Matthew," Pew said. "But ye have not told me thy life's vocation. Only that ye both be musicians: a drummer, the one; the other a bass violist."

"That's what we do, Abner," I told him. "We're professional musicians."

"That is no profession." Pew sneered. "'Tis a pastime: a mere divertissement."

"Now you sound like my father," Matty said.

"Thy sire would be a wise man, from the sound of him," Pew said seriously. "And idle badinage does not speed thy purpose of escape from the hue and cry that will soon follow ye. I shall therefore select a proper era for ye both. Tell me, do ye still have in thy possession the key which I gave ye?" he asked.

"Right here, Abner," I said, producing it from my pocket.

"'Tis well ye have guarded it carefully. It be the instrument of thy return to the future. Remember the recipe for its proper use. Now ye must perform the ritual."

Matty and I went through the required drill to enter the

gate to the past. We stood at the foot of Pew's tombstone, facing it. Then we took two paces toward it, turned, and began to walk away. We felt a momentary chill, then found ourselves standing in the graveyard, in broad daylight. And it was cold outside, too.

We had to be in some winter month. It was a good thing that when we'd been in 1942, it was wintertime. The clothes we had on were uncomfortable in June of 1912, but now I was glad for the ratty, threadbear overcoat I wore. Although I felt it was winter, I didn't know what year it was.

"Pew!" I called out. "What year is this?"

"It be the year 1906, the month of January. I wish thee well, young squire, in the search for the gate."

"Thanks, Abner," I said to the crisp air of the January morning. Then Matty and I exchanged glances, as if to say *What now?* He made a bow and did an after-you gesture. I nodded back, and we began walking.

I have to laugh when I hear commuters in 1976 talk about how it only takes them an hour or so to get to New York from Branford. It took Matty and me two days. We got a couple of rides with farmers on chicken wagons. Wagons pulled by horses, not trucks. We rode in the back with the birds. It was a good thing the weather was cold. The smell from the chickens was fierce, and clung to our clothing, once we got indoors.

But, finally, we made it to Manhattan. What a shock! When we visited New York City in 1942, it wasn't too much different from our own time. But in 1906, it was a whole other place, as they say.

Our biggest problem was food. We couldn't spend the fifty-cent piece Mrs. Gilchrist had given us. It was dated

1912. On top of that, it was colder than the North Pole, and we had no place to stay. Down around Sixth Street, on the East Side, we lucked out, though.

Standing on a corner, in the cold, was a four-piece brass band: two cornets, a baritone horn, and a trombone. The band all wore uniforms: black with blue piping and matching caps. There were also two women, dressed in female versions of the uniform, but instead of caps, they wore bonnets. There was a tripod with an iron kettle over it, nearby. No fire under it, though. It was for people to put coins in. I knew that because I saw a man in a business suit drop a penny in it as he passed by. A sign over the tripod read: *Give to the Guiding Light Rescue Mission. Save a Soul!*

Matty nudged me and nodded his head at the band. "I think I've got us a hot meal, pal," he said. "If these folks are like the Salvation Army, they feed hungry sinners."

"Matty, you wouldn't..." I said.

"Oh, wouldn't I?" he replied.

We walked up to the little band just as the two women burst into song. It was "Rock of Ages." They weren't bad, either. Matty and I stood there, shifting from foot to foot in the cold. Funny thing with me and music. It always takes the sting out of things when I'm in bad shape. Matty was digging it, too. When they finished the tune, the lady who'd been singing soprano noticed the attention we'd been paying to their little concert.

She was wearing that uniform and bonnet, but anyone could see she was one fine-looking lady. She had incredibly clear blue eyes, and skin that glowed in the chill air. She gave Matty and me a beautiful smile and said to us, "Have you been saved?"

Matty stepped forward. "Yes, sister," he said in a phony, trembling voice, "I have, but I have strayed into evil ways. I have no work....I haven't eaten in three days. I feel the urge to..." He looked over both shoulders, as though he was about to let the Rescue Mission lady in on some big secret. "...To *steal* food!" he whispered so loud you could hear him ten feet away. Then, with this, he fell at her feet in the phoniest faint I've seen since Saturday-morning cartoons!

Suddenly, the pretty Rescue Mission lady was all business. She dropped to her knees next to Matty and cradled his head in her arms. She looked over her shoulder at the band and the other Rescue Mission lady. "Pack up the band, Sister Matilda," she commanded. "We must get this poor man to the shelter and feed him." She looked up at me and said, "You are his companion?"

"Yes, ma'am," I replied.

"Then help me with him," she cried, "or have you forgotten how to be a Christian?"

I went to where Matty lay, got my arms under his shoulders, and hauled him to his feet. What an actor. He didn't even help me. With the Rescue Mission lady helping from the other side, we began walking Matty down Bowery Street, the band and Sister Matilda trailing behind.

"Where are we going?" I asked the lady.

"Just to Fifth Street," she grunted, struggling with Matty's weight. "Our mission is there....Your friend is rather heavy, for a near-starved man."

Matty fluttered his eyes then and groaned. He began to take a few weak steps, taking some of the weight off me and the lady. It worked. She forgot about how heavy my "starving" pal was and said, "Hurry! He needs food!"

I'd like to feed him a knuckle sandwich, I thought....

I felt like a rat doing it, but we stayed at the mission for almost two weeks. As soon as Sister Amelia (it turned out that was the pretty lady's name) found out we were musicians, that cinched it. We played with the mission band, and stayed in their shelter. The food was plain but good. The beds were hard but clean.

What wasn't clean was my conscience. We'd conned the nice lady. And I guess my Catholic upbringing was stronger than I'd thought. The whole idea of taking food and shelter on false pretenses was like lying to any clergyperson. You just don't do that. To make it all the more complicated, Sister Amelia started hinting around about Matty and me becoming permanent members of the Guiding Light Rescue Mission. She wanted to have us fitted out with uniforms, like the rest of the band. That's when I drew the line.

"I just can't keep doing it, Matty," I said one night. We were lying in the darkness of the dormitory, with drunks and derelicts snoring all around us. "We have to leave here."

"And go where?" Matty asked. "At least we have a warm place to stay, and we're eating regularly. Sister Amelia's happy with us. We have some brand-new clothes she gave us...."

"And we're no closer to finding the future gate than we were two weeks ago," I put in.

"True," he agreed, "but now we're in shape to start looking. Maybe if we stayed here until the weather got warmer?"

That's when I told Matty what was really on my mind. About how I couldn't go on lying to Sister Amelia. That every mouthful of food I took made me feel a bigger rat. "And I just can't keep doing it, Matty," I finished.

"I have to think about this, Richie," Matty said. "Your conscience is one thing. The cold weather outside is another."

"Well, think of it this way," I said. "If we don't tell the truth to Sister Amelia and give her our deepest apologies this weekend, I'm going to leave by myself."

"You really mean it, don't you?"

"You bet your neck," I said. Except I didn't say *neck*.

And that's just what we did. I told Sister Amelia as much of the story as I could without her calling an ambulance to put me in a rubber room at a laughing academy. Matty even told her that his faint on the street had been phony. Sister Amelia only smiled.

"I knew that," she said.

"What?" we both said at the same time.

"Certainly," Sister Amelia said. "I knew it as soon as I felt how heavy Matthew was. He was hardly wasting away from hunger, you know."

I felt my face growing red. Matty looked down at his feet as though he'd just discovered them there, at the end of his ankles.

"However," Sister Amelia went on, "the both of you have been excellent soldiers for the two weeks you've been here. You have done the Lord's work, and I assure you, it was well appreciated. Not just by me, but by Him who will come to judge us all, someday. I would never presume to question your motives. 'Judge not, lest ye be judged,'" she quoted.

"I don't know what to say..." Matty began.

"A simple thank-you would be adequate, Matthew," she said.

"Thank you, Sister Amelia," Matty mumbled. "I feel like a fool."

"We are all fools, each of us, in his time," she said.

"Is that a quote?" I asked.

"It is indeed," she replied. "My father, Colonel Smith, who founded this mission, said it often. He passed away just last year."

"I'm sorry," I said.

"For what?" Sister Amelia asked. "He is now in heaven, with the Lord...." She paused and looked hard at the two of us. "Yet, before he died, he told me something like this might happen one day. That I would meet two young men, one white, one colored, who needed help. He also said that you two, somehow, were responsible for the work of the mission continuing. I thought it was delirium when he said all this on his deathbed. Yet here you are. I don't pretend to understand. But here...take this, as well."

She held out her hand and gave us a dollar bill. It was bigger by a third than any dollar bill I'd ever seen, but undoubtedly good 1906-type spending money. That got to Matty.

"We'll pay it back, with interest, Sister," he said, with what might have been tears in his eyes.

"No need," she said. "Just live your life as a good, sober Christian, Matthew. That will be repayment enough. Now, goodbye, and may God bless you both."

"Thank you, Sister," I said. Then to Matty, I said in a low voice, "Come on, you silver-tongued con man. Let's go find a job." As we walked out the door of the mission, I looked back for a second. She was still there, smiling.

We walked in silence, all the way up to Fourteenth Street. Matty felt lower than a snake's sneakers, I'm sure. I was thinking my own thoughts about what a swell person Sister Amelia was. I was also puzzled about the way people were helping us. Then I figured that maybe in 1906 and 1912, people were less cold than in my own time.

Suddenly, Matty grabbed my arm. "Richie!" he cried. "I've got it!"

"I hope what you got ain't catching," I grumbled. "I'm fed up with your slick ideas, pal."

"No, Richie," he said hurriedly, "not a scam. This is legit. I just now thought of someone in 1906 who'd listen to our story. A guy we could tell the whole truth to. And he might be the one person who'd help us find the gate."

"Swell," I said without enthusiasm. "Who do you have in mind? Sherlock Holmes?"

"No, my man," Matty said, pointing to a nearby wall. "Him."

I followed his pointed finger with my eyes. There on the side of a building was plastered a full-color poster, reading:

NOW APPEARING AT HAMMERSTEIN'S
VICTORIA THEATER:
THE GREAT HOUDINI!

4

Houdini

"Houdini, huh?" I asked. "What makes you think he could help us? Or even be interested?"

"He's got to be. Didn't you see that movie of his life, on TV?"

"Sure I did. What of it?"

"Well, in the flick, Houdini was into all that occult stuff...strange happenings and all."

"Matty, that was just a movie. You know movie biographies aren't necessarily true to life. I think you're grabbing at straws."

"I gotta grab at something, Richie. Are you with me?"

"I've been with you this far. Let's start walking. It's over a mile to Times Square, where the Victoria Theater is."

On the way, we figured out how we were going to get an interview with Houdini. We thought we could leave a message at the stage door or ask an usher at the theater to bring him a note. Man, talk about not knowing your way around!

The Victoria was a mob scene. We hadn't realized that Houdini was one of the most popular entertainers in the world in 1906. You could no more get a note to him than you could to Elton John or the Rolling Stones in 1976. The alleyway to the stage door was wall-to-wall people. That left Plan B. Get a note to an usher, inside the theater. And the line for tickets ran all the way around the block.

"It doesn't look good, Matty," I said. "Did you see that sign?" I pointed to a hand-lettered card on a tripod in front of the box office. It read: *Matinee Performance Sold Out. Tickets on Sale for Evening Performance Only.*

"It's worse than that, brother," Matty said. "Look at that admission price. A buck and a half. That's almost a day's pay in 1906."

"Well, so much for that idea," I said glumly. "We can't afford the tickets. How can we get to Houdini?"

"I think I have it," Matty said. "Look at that poster over there. It says that Houdini accepts all challenges to confine him."

"Yeah, we both know that."

"But look at the bottom of the poster," Matty insisted. "It says that challenges have to be delivered in advance to Houdini's office, at 278 West 113th Street. That's where we'll go."

"Right now?" I asked. "He won't be there until tomorrow morning. Or maybe someone else handles the challenges."

"Face it," Matty said, "we don't have anyplace else to go, do we? We can camp on his doorstep until he shows up. Come on, Richie. Put on your walking shoes. It's a long hike to 113th Street."

There are about twenty city blocks to the mile. We had walked to Times Square from Fourteenth Street. That was nearly a mile and a half. The hike to 113th made it another four. Maybe we could have splurged and taken a streetcar, but we had to save what money we had for eating.

When we got to 278 West 113th Street, all of a sudden my feet didn't hurt near as much. I'd expected to find an office building, but number 278 was a private residence. A brownstone, three floors high, in a row of similar buildings.

"Talk about luck!" I crowed to Matty. "He lives here! All we have to do now is wait until he shows up after the last show. He's bound to come home some time!"

That he did. At about one o'clock in the morning. Matty and I were nearly frozen like Popsicles. We'd taken turns waiting, each of us walking to a drugstore three blocks away to drink coffee at the counter and warm up a bit. Or I should say that *I* drank coffee at the counter. They wouldn't serve Matty. He could buy it to go, but couldn't drink it on the premises. Welcome to liberal New York, circa 1906.

Houdini and company pulled up in front of the building in a horse-drawn cab. There was no mistaking the great escape artist from his pictures on the posters. But I was shocked to see how short he was! He couldn't have been more than five foot five. But I guess everyone looks big on posters. Like when you see a movie star, you expect him to be the same size he was on the screen. Anyway, Houdini turned out to be real little.

He got out of the cab and helped this beautiful, dark-haired lady from the vehicle. She was even shorter than Houdini, and the two small people made the six-foot-tall man in his thirties who was with them look like a giant. As they headed toward the door to number 278, I went into action. Matty and I had worked it all out during the long, cold wait.

"Mr. Houdini!" I called out. "I have a challenge for you!"

"It's Houdini—not mister, professor, or anything like it," said the tallish man, getting between me and the magician immediately. "There is only one Houdini. There is no need for an honorific. And any business you wish to do will be handled during office hours, young man. I am Houdini's secretary...."

I realized what was going on, almost too late. The tallish man was stalling me while Houdini and the pretty lady were going up the stone steps of the 113th Street house.

"Wait, Houdini, wait!" I called out. "I can read the future. I have been in the future, and I have proof of it!"

The magician stopped abruptly. He turned and looked at me with an incredibly intense stare from blue eyes as cold as ice. He may have been a half a foot shorter than me, but he had a compelling gaze. You knew from the way he held himself and looked at you that you were dealing with someone *important:* a real star.

"You can prove these words to Houdini?" he said, speaking for the first time. He had a heavy New York accent. "Words" came out *woids.*

"I have undeniable proof, Houdini," I replied.

"Have him come in, Sargeant," Houdini said to the tallish man. To me, he said, "Mr. Sargeant will interview you. If your claim is true, in his opinion, I will receive you."

"I have a friend with me, Houdini," I said, and waved Matty from out of a nearby doorway. Neither one of us liked the idea of Matty hiding, but this might be our only chance. If nobody would listen to him, we decided that I had to do the talking.

Houdini swept his icy gaze over Matty, seeming to take

in every detail in an instant. "Very well," he said; then, with the small lady, he went inside the house. Mr. Sargeant looked us up and down.

"This had better be very good, indeed," he said. "Come with me, you two."

He led us into a sitting room that was set up as an office. He sat at a chair alongside a huge desk and waved Matty and me to a big leather couch that sat against the far wall. I noticed he didn't sit behind the desk. It must have been the great man's personal preserve.

He took a lined pad from the top of the desk and produced a gold mechanical pencil from inside his coat, which he'd unbuttoned to display full evening dress: white tie and tails. Matty and I took off our overcoats so we wouldn't catch a chill when we went outside again.

"I am John W. Sargeant, Houdini's secretary and assistant," he said in a resonant voice. "And you two are remarkably lucky to have this hearing. However, all one need do is mention the weird or bizarre to Houdini to get his ear. To be able to prove it is another matter. Now, as to the particulars of your claim..."

"It's not a claim, sir," I said. "I am actually from the future. I've found a way to travel in time. I was born in New York in 1958. I am eighteen years old. It was in 1976 that I found the way to travel backward in time. My friend, too."

Sargeant didn't even raise an eyebrow. "Your name?" he asked.

"Gilroy. Richard Gilroy. My friend is Matthew Owen."

"Your addresses?"

"Just now, we don't have an address. We're strangers to this time."

"And what proof do you have of this fantastic tale?" he asked.

That's when I played my trump card. I mean, put yourself in my place. How would *you* prove it? Tell the man about World War I, which wouldn't happen for another eight years? It would take too long to prove it.

Matty knew gangs of stuff about sports, but that was no good to us either. Any prediction he could make would require us to wait months or years to prove he was right. And Sargeant wanted proof right now. Luckily, we had it.

"Here's all the proof you'll need," I said, and put in his hand the fifty-cent piece Mrs. Gilchrist had given us in 1912.

Sargeant looked the coin over carefully. Luckily, I once collected coins and knew what to say. "As you can see, Mr. Sargeant," I said, "the coin is genuine. It has the mark of the Denver mint. It's not a refinished or tampered-with coin. It's been circulated, and the date of 1912 stamped on it has the same amount of wear as the rest of it."

Sargeant held up a hand for silence. He went behind the desk and opened a drawer. He took out a magnifying glass and held the coin under the desk lamp while he examined it more closely. The lamp was electric, I noted, although there were what appeared to be working gas lighting fixtures on the walls and ceiling of the room. After a few minutes that seemed like hours to Matty and me, he stood up abruptly.

"Wait right here," he said shortly, and left the room, closing the door behind him. I heard the lock click shut. He wasn't taking any chances on leaving a couple of guys who looked like we did along with all the expensive stuff in the office. He was gone for some time.

"Do you think Houdini'll see us?" Matty asked me.

"I think so. The coin's genuine. Anyone can see that."

"But Sargeant's been gone a long time," Matty protested. "Maybe he's calling the cops or something."

"What for? We didn't do anything."

"We didn't do anything in 1912 or 1942, either, but look at the trouble we had."

I never got a chance to answer that one. A key rattled in the door, and Sargeant stood in the open doorway. "Houdini will see you," he announced. The great man, wearing a silk robe over his formal shirt and white tie, strode into the room with all the authority of Napoleon inspecting his troops. Matty and I couldn't help it, we both stood up. Houdini nodded to us like a king and went and sat behind his desk. Sargeant sat in the chair he'd been using before. He waved at us to approach him.

"Now, what's all this bunkum about the future?" Houdini demanded. "And how did you make this half a buck?"

5

The House of Magic

It took us hours to convince Houdini we were telling the truth. I don't mind saying that if I was in his place, I wouldn't have been convinced so easy. But it was just like Sargeant had told us. Houdini *wanted* to believe in the strange and oddball things he read and heard of. Maybe when your stock in trade is illusion, you like to believe that somewhere, somehow, there really is magic in the world. Trouble is, once Houdini did accept what we said as truth, we couldn't answer a tenth of the questions he asked about the future.

It was all because we were just ordinary young guys in 1976. If you think about it, how much does the average high school student know about history? And neither one of us was that good in history to begin with. Maybe if we talked history of jazz, we wouldn't have come off so dumb. Even so, the jazz we knew about wasn't going to develop for another twenty years or so. Houdini kept at us, though.

"Now, this world war that begins in 1914," Houdini asked, "can you tell me how it started? I've recently toured Europe, including Germany and Austria. There's no threat of war that I could see."

I wracked my brain, trying to remember what I could of World War I. "It was on account of German submarines sinking the *Lusitania*," I said.

"The *Lusitania?*" Houdini asked. "The brand-new Cunard liner? It's unsinkable!" he snapped. "So is the sister ship, the *Mauretania.*"

"Not when you put a torpedo below the waterline," Matty said. "The *Lusitania* blew up."

"But it's a passenger ship, not a warship," Houdini protested. "And it's British. Why would a German ship want to sink it? And how would that get us into a war with Germany?"

"American passengers on board," I replied.

"I can't believe it," Houdini said, shaking his head. "We have excellent diplomatic relations with Germany."

"Tell that to Kaiser Wilhelm II," I said. "He wanted the war, my history teacher said."

"That I can understand," Houdini said. "I've met the Kaiser. He's an arrogant so-and-so."

It went on like that for most of the night—Houdini asking us about everything under the sun, and us doing our best to answer his questions. Mr. Sargeant went out of the room and came back with coffee and sandwiches a couple of times. Matty and I wolfed them down, but Houdini only sipped at ice water. Finally, he came to a part of the conversation I'd been dreading, but I had to expect. His own future.

Now, I happen to know, from the flick I saw, when and how Houdini died. It's easy to remember, really. He died on Halloween in 1926. But when Houdini asked about himself, I avoided the date.

"You'll always be remembered in history as the greatest

magician and escape artist the world has ever known," I told him.

"Houdini is that right now," the little man said smugly. I had to admit he was right. "Tell me more about my future," he urged.

"Your present reputation is just the beginning, Houdini," I continued. "Years from now, people will still be talking about the way you walked through walls, how you escaped from milk cans filled with water...your Chinese water torture escape..."

"Just a second," Houdini said, holding up an imperious hand. "I'm already doing the walk-through-walls gag. But this milk can and...what'd you call it? The Chinese water torture? I never *hoid* of such gags!"

"Maybe you haven't done it yet," I explained. "Like I told you, I know a lot about what'll happen in the future. But I'm shaky on dates and such...."

"Are you getting all this down in shorthand, Sargeant?" Houdini asked.

"Every word, Houdini," the man replied.

"Good," he said, then turned back to me. "Now, Richie," he said, "describe these stunts to me. All you can remember about them."

I told him about the Chinese water cell, where the magician escapes from a tank of water while he's hanging upside down, chained hand and foot. "But I have no idea how it's done," I concluded.

"That's awright, kid," Houdini said with a warm smile, "*Houdini* knows. Or I will know. I think I know already. It's a variation on a gag I used to do with a trunk underwater. Now tell me about these milk cans."

I did, as best I could. The assistants get an oversized

old-fashioned milk can and fill it with water. The magician gets inside it, with handcuffs on. Then the lid is put on and locked with any padlock the audience wants to provide.

"Wait a sec," Houdini said. "You say the locks come from out of the audience?"

"Yep. Then the assistants draw curtains around the can for five minutes while the band plays. I couldn't help it, I tried holding my breath when I saw the trick."

Houdini laughed out loud: a boyish, high-pitched laugh that surprised me. "That's what the magician wants you to do," he said, "hold your breath. I bet you that in five minutes, he shows up from behind the curtains dripping wet. And the locks on the milk can ain't been touched, right?"

"How did you know?" I asked.

"Figured it out while you were telling me about it. It's so simple, it's brilliant!"

"You should know, Houdini," Matty put in. "It's your idea."

"Yeah, it *is*, isn't it?" he said, grinning broadly. He rubbed his hands together. "I can hardly wait to get going on these gags. I've been looking for something to punch up the act. Sargeant, get the workshop staff ready. I'm going to start making work sketches first thing tomorrow."

"Yes, Houdini," the man said, and made a note of it.

Then Houdini returned his attention to me. "I owe you boys for these swell ideas," he said. "Or maybe I don't— if, like you say, history says I invented them.

"And I'm fascinated by your gates in time, boys," he added. "We must find this future gate you talked about. The directions this Pew guy gave you...they're pretty vague."

"Don't we know it?" Matty said. "But anywhere there's a gate, someone is going to report a strange thing or event happening. Like I'm sure that the guy who almost shot us in the graveyard in 1942 told somebody about us disappearing in front of his eyes."

"Don't be too sure, Matty," Houdini said. "Many people have strange experiences that they never talk about. They're afraid people will think they're crazy. But you two are in luck. I keep a file of strange happenings. I have people all over the world who send me anything unusual that happens to them, or that's in any newspaper. I owe you two. You can go through my files and see if anyone has reported an occurrence that might indicate a future gate. The files are upstairs, in boxes. They may take you weeks to read, though."

"We'll be back first thing tomorrow," I said.

Houdini laughed and drew back the curtains from the window behind his desk. Bright daylight streamed in. "It *is* tomorrow," he said. "And what's all this gab about coming back? You told me you don't have anywhere to live. You stay with Houdini. I won't let you stay anyplace else. I have too much more to ask you. Sargeant will take you to a guest room. You don't mind sharing a room, do you?"

I thought about the choice places we'd been staying at lately, and said, "No, not at all."

"Good, good," Houdini said. He stood up. "Now, I must rest awhile and prepare. I have a matinee performance in five hours."

"You won't get much sleep," Matty said.

The great magician drew himself up to his full five feet five inches. "Houdini has absolute control of his bodily functions," he said. "Houdini never sleeps more than five hours. He can hold his breath for more than three minutes. Should he choose, Houdini can go without sleep for days."

"Well, Matty Owen can't," Matty cracked. "I'm going to bed."

"Me, too," I said. "And I can't thank you enough, Houdini."

Houdini only nodded, and walked toward the door. Sargeant opened it for him, and the little man strode through it like he was an emperor. No matter how little he was, Houdini carried himself like a giant. And I suppose that in his field, that's just what he was. I have to admit he impressed me. Even if he did say *woid, thoid,* and *boid.*

At three o'clock that afternoon, Matty and I had eaten a very late brunch and were going over Houdini's files of strange happenings. As he'd said, he kept the files in a bunch of boxes on the third floor of his townhouse.

The townhouse was something else, too. Houdini had a mania for collecting stuff. A lot of it was made up of old paintings and engravings of magicians from the past. It seemed that anything that had to do with the magical arts he'd bought.

Sargeant also showed us Houdini's personal bathroom. That might not sound like an item on a tour, but you had to see it. It was marble, with gold fixtures, and had his initials HH set into it. It was also big enough that Matty and I could have both used it at the same time. Sargeant explained that Houdini used the tub not just for bathing, but for practicing holding his breath underwater. Even when this guy took a bath, he kept working to make his act better!

The files on oddball events were huge. We began with *A* and went at it for hours. Some of the items had to be made up, we decided. They were too crazy to be true.

"Look at this, Richie," Matty said, holding up a yellowed newspaper item. "A guy in Detroit burst into flames."

"Smoking in bed?"

"Nah. He was in a hotel room, and he was with someone. The guy all of a sudden catches fire. Only his shoes left. And nothing else in the room was even scorched."

"Far out," I said. "Somebody made that up."

"Not if you read the article. The guy who was with him was a minister, and he swears that's what happened."

"I got one here that looks good," I said. "A couple of ladies from England were visiting Paris during the big exposition. The one they built the Eiffel Tower for. Seems they walked around some hedges in a park and disappeared."

"You can do that in any big city," Matty said.

"Didn't work that way," I came back. "The park was fenced and had guards at the gates. It seems they charge you to go into parks in Paris. No one saw them leave. No one saw them after they walked around the hedges."

"When did this happen?"

"Nearly twenty years ago, I think. I can't make out the date."

"It sounds like a gate," Matty said. "Make a note of it."

And so it went. Item after item, page after page. I never knew so many weird things went on in the world. Trouble was, almost all these goofy things happened long ago, or in places in the world we could never afford to go to: Paris, Rome, India, and China. We kept plugging away, though. When Sargeant came to the door of the room we were researching in, neither one of us had noticed how late it had gotten. We hadn't eaten dinner, and Houdini was already back from the Victoria. Sargeant brought us downstairs to Houdini's office.

He'd changed into his silk robe and was sitting behind his huge desk when we entered. He looked up as we came in with Sargeant.

"How goes the *resoich?*" he asked.

"Not too good, Houdini," I said. "We haven't read a tenth of the stuff you have on file."

"It doesn't matter," Houdini said with a bright grin. He had a very warm and charming smile, for all his aggressive manner. He pushed a newspaper item toward us across the desk. "Look at that," he said proudly. "If I'm not mistaken, and I hardly ever am, I think I've found your gate."

It was a copy of the *San Francisco Examiner,* dated January 1, 1906. Just a month ago. "The item is on page fifteen," Houdini said, "last column on the right." It was only a few paragraphs, but as I read on, with Matty looking over my shoulder, both of us grew more and more excited.

STRANGE EVENTS IN GOLDEN GATE PARK

January 1—Perhaps our populace has been celebrating the New Year with more zeal than usual. On this morning, one J. Gavin, a soap salesman of our fair city, accompanied by a lady who was unidentified, encountered a man in the garb of a Spanish *conquistador.*

Believing the man to be a late-night reveler from a fancy dress ball, Gavin offered the man in armor a libation from the flask he carried on his hip. The man in armor replied in Spanish. Gavin felt this was carrying the jest too far. He tried to jolly the "Spaniard" into a nip.

To his horror, and that of his female companion, the armored man drew a sword and wounded Gavin in the left shoulder. He then fled and hid behind an outcropping of rock. When Gavin arrived, hot on his heels, the "Spaniard" had unaccountably vanished. At least, that's Mr. Gavin's tale.

We are of the opinion that the whiskey being poured in the Golden Gate Park area is a good deal better than it is reputed to be.

"That's it!" Matty hollered. "The guy really was from the past. He had to be! Especially the way he vanished. He came from the past, into 1906, then went back again. He wasn't here long enough to get stuck! That's where our future gate is: San Francisco, in Golden Gate Park!"

"Or the guy was coming from a Spanish-speaking party on New Year's morning," I said.

"I side with Matty," Houdini said. "All the parts and descriptions seem to fit."

"Then I only have one question," I said.

"And that is?" Houdini asked.

"When does the next flight...er, *train* leave for San Francisco?"

"That's not my question," Matty said. "Mine is, how do we come up with train fare? We're broke, or almost. We have sixty-five cents, bro."

"I guess we have to count on you, Houdini," I said.

An abrupt change came over the little man's face. As though I'd slapped him in the chops. He got up from his desk and began to walk up and down in front of Matty and me.

"That's the trouble with people today," he said. "Always with their hands out. Do you know what this house cost me? Do you know what it costs to run? Do you think Houdini can change lead into gold? If you want to get to California, you'll have to *woik* for it." He gestured to Sargeant. "When is Manfred going out on the Western circuit?" he asked.

"In a week's time, Houdini."

"Get these two jobs with him. Assistants...porters. I don't care what. Manfred owes me. Hell, he *woiks* for me!" Houdini looked up at Matty and me and smiled. "Awright," he said. "I'll get you to San Francisco."

6

Manfred the Great Meets
Matty the Prince

"Who's Manfred?" I asked of Sargeant after Houdini had
left the room.

"He's a magician," Sargeant replied. "A sort of protégé
of Houdini's. He doesn't get star billing, the way Houdini
does. He's good enough at what he does, but he lacks
Houdini's personality. He also lacks a real act. Now, Houdini will do some stage illusions, like the brick wall gag, or
manipulate cards. But his real act is a thing he invented
himself: the escape. Before Houdini, no one had ever built
an entire act around escaping. He's made it an art form.
Now any guy who has the price of a set of handcuffs is
billing himself as an escape artist.

"Manfred—his real name is Fred Mann, by the way—
has an act made of a few card tricks, some illusions, and
some escapes. He tries to cover it all, and in consequence,
he doesn't do anything really well."

"Then what's his connection with Houdini?" I asked.

"Well, Manfred is Mrs. Houdini's second cousin," Sargeant said. "He was an insurance salesman and failed at
it. He had a haberdashery in Brooklyn for a time, and that
failed. But he's a handsome man, and figured he'd try his

hand at the show business. Being distantly related to Bess Houdini, he asked a favor of her. After all, he saw Houdini's brother Theo set up in the magic game as Hardeen. Why not Fred Mann as Manfred the Great?"

"If he's not so hot at the magic game, why did Houdini do it?"

"Family ties are very important to Houdini," Sargeant said. "And he'd do anything in the world for his wife, Bess. They've been married for years now, and they still act like newlyweds."

"And we're going to work for Manfred?"

"That's what Houdini said. And when Houdini says something, it has a way of coming to pass."

"What cities will we be working?" I asked.

"I'm not certain of his total bookings," Sargeant said. "But I do know that Manfred will play a week in Buffalo, a week in Cleveland, then another two weeks in Detroit and Chicago. From there, his tour will take him to San Francisco. He should be there the last week in March or the first week in April. After that, he swings down to Los Angeles: a minor booking. Then he works his way back east via the southern route."

"As long as we get to Frisco, it's okay with me," Matty said.

Sargeant took a watch from his vest pocket. "It's after two in the morning, boys," he said. "Unlike Houdini, I require some sleep occasionally. I'll wake you at eight; we'll meet with Manfred here at nine. He has some things he must pick up from Houdini's workshop."

"Where's that?" Matty asked.

"He has a large one, downtown," Sargeant said, "but he has a smaller, more secret one downstairs in this house.

Manfred will be coming here." He paused. "Uh...I think it best you don't tell Manfred who you are and where you come from," he said. "He is a relative of Houdini's by marriage, but I don't feel he should know any more than is absolutely necessary."

"Gotcha," Matty said.

"Also," Sargeant added, "you should be ready in time to leave with Manfred. Now I bid you both good night." He left the room, and Matty and I looked at each other and smiled.

"We did it, Richie," Matty said. "We got our ticket to San Francisco!"

"I dunno," I said. "Has it occurred to you that we're in deep trouble if the gate *isn't* in San Francisco?"

"Come on, Richie. You read the newspaper article. The gate *has* to be there."

"Okay, okay. I'm just saying that if it isn't, we better have a standby plan."

"Let's deal with it when it happens," Matty said. "Come on, let's turn in. We have an early day tomorrow."

Manfred the Great, or Fred Mann, *looked* like a stage magician. He was everything Houdini wasn't. He was quite tall, over six feet, and had dark hair slicked back from a widow's peak. He had a mustache and a pointy, devil's beard. When he showed up at Houdini's house, he was wearing a dark coat, striped trousers, a pale vest, and a wing-collar shirt with an ascot tie. There was a diamond stickpin in the tie.

Instead of an overcoat, he wore a cape with a red satin lining. The entire ensemble was topped off by a high silk hat and a silver-headed walking stick. As he entered, he tossed his hat, cape, and cane at Sargeant. Houdini wasn't there. He had a matinee at the Victoria and some early business downtown to see to.

"Ah there, Sargeant," Manfred said in a rich basso voice. "You're looking your usual overworked self today." Manfred scanned the room with a piercing, dark-eyed glance, taking in Matty and me. "I assume these are the two supers Houdini wants me to hire?" he asked, then frowned. "You didn't say one of them was a colored boy."

"You didn't ask," Sargeant said. "And besides, what difference does it make? If Houdini says they're on the payroll, they are."

"You are not an *artiste*, Sargeant," Manfred said, real snotty. "The colored boy presents a problem."

"The *colored boy* has a name," Matty put in. "I'm Matty Owen. This is my friend, Richie Gilroy."

"Delighted," Manfred said, in a tone of voice he'd use if somebody offered him a wormburger. He didn't extend his hand for a shake, but continued talking to Sargeant. "Tell me this, Sargeant," he said, "how does the colored ...er, Matty travel? Where does he stay? Railroads and hotels, even theatrical boarding houses, have their standards."

"Don't crap me, Manfred," Sargeant said. "You hadn't stayed at a hotel in your entire life until Houdini took you in. I also happen to know that you stay at boarding houses whenever you can. They're cheaper than hotels, and they serve meals. Also, they don't complain about your parties and drinking after the show."

"Uh...quite so," Manfred the Great said, a flush of red at his wing collar. He evidently had been trying to impress me and Matty. But Sargeant wasn't letting him get away

with it. In a flash, I saw why Manfred wasn't big-time, even
if he looked good. He didn't have Houdini's charisma, or
half his class. Manfred walked into a room and demanded
respect in a loud voice. Houdini entered a room and *commanded* respect, without saying a word.

"But you must understand," Manfred insisted, "that
traveling with this Owen boy *will* pose problems, Sargeant."

"Which I am sure you'll solve, Manfred," Sargeant answered. "I know you will, because Houdini has made his
wishes clear on the subject. Face it, Fred. You wouldn't
have any equipment, wardrobe, or even an act if you
weren't Bess Houdini's cousin. Now it's time to pay back
your debts to Houdini. As if you ever *could.*"

Manfred hemmed and hawed, cleared his throat, and
finally said, "Well, I suppose something could be worked
out."

"That's the spirit, Manfred," Sargeant said, getting up
and clapping the magician on the shoulder. As though he
hadn't made crap of the man just a few seconds before.

I was beginning to see that John Sargeant was far from
being Houdini's doormat. In his own way, Sargeant was a
powerful and ruthless man. I'd seen what he'd done to
Manfred, and I didn't want to be on the receiving end
from Sargeant, ever. He was more than Houdini's secretary. He was his administrator and his hatchet man.

"Now I want you to take these boys downtown with you.
Get them some decent clothes. You'll find stage costumes
for them downstairs, in Houdini's storeroom," Sargeant
told Manfred.

"Houdini wants them *onstage?*" Manfred said in a shocked
voice. "Never! I will not work with amateurs!"

"Your budget calls for two items of hired help, Fred,"

Sargeant said impatiently. "You need one assistant onstage and one porter to handle props, luggage, and hecklers. One of the boys will assist you; the other will fetch and carry."

"Guess who gets to fetch and carry," Matty whispered to me.

"But they're *untrained!*" Manfred wailed.

"Then you have a week in which to train them, Fred," said Sargeant with an airy wave of his hand. "You'd better get started now. They'll be staying with you at the Belvedere Hotel. If that's where you're really staying."

"I beg your pardon," Manfred said huffily.

"Oh, drop it, will you, Fred?" Sargeant said. "For all I know, you're staying at Ma Reilly's boarding house and charging Houdini for the Belvedere. You have someone give you a blank bill. Or worse, you swipe a blank and then have Houdini pay it."

"I assure you, Sargeant, I am staying at the Belvedere. And tell me, how do I get *him* in?" He pointed a long, bony finger at Matty.

Sargeant sat there and made his fingers into a little tent. In a minute, he stood up and sighed heavily. "Come downstairs with me," he said. "I have an idea."

Matty looked at himself in the cheval mirror in the downstairs storeroom. He burst into raucous laughter. I couldn't help it; I did, too. He looked ridiculous. He had on yellow satin baggy pants, pointy-toed slippers with turned-up ends, and a green satin jacket over a puffy-sleeved white silk shirt. The whole outfit was topped off by a white turban. In the middle of the turban was a phony red jewel, and growing out of it, straight up, was a silly peacock feather!

Evidently this weird getup was some American costume designer's idea of what an Indian potentate looked like.

"Now, Matty," Sargeant said, "if you can't do the accent properly, don't even try it. Don't say anything in public."

"Don't worry about my dialect, *sahib*," Matty said in an accent that sounded Polish to me. "No one will hear my accent. The suit is too loud!"

"You only need wear it onstage," Sargeant said, ignoring Matty's joke. "But you had better wear the turban at all times. Wait here. I may have some extra turbans." He went back to the long racks, loaded with all kinds of getups.

"Try to find one without that fruity feather in it, will you?" Matty asked.

Sargeant came back with three other turbans. Happily for Matty, they were plain white, with no extras on them. Sargeant also handed a wrapped package to Manfred. "Here's the new set of springs for the metamorphosis box, Manfred," he told the magician.

I wanted to ask what a metamorphosis box was, but I figured I'd find out later. Sargeant also dug up an old cardboard suitcase to keep the stuff in. We followed him upstairs and back into Houdini's office. Sargeant went behind Houdini's desk, opened a drawer, and took out a steel cashbox. He opened it with a key that hung on his watch chain. He took out a couple of bills.

"You'll need cash for expenses and meals," he said to Matty and me. "Here is a five-dollar bill for each of you. That's a week's pay in advance. After this, a dollar a week will be deducted from your salaries until your advance is paid back. Now I have work to do for Houdini. I wish you both the best of luck."

We shook hands with Sargeant and left with Manfred

the Great. Manfred said that to get through the lobby of the Belvedere, Matty ought to be fully costumed.

I smiled at the irony of the situation. Matty, as an ordinary black man, woudn't be allowed to stay at the hotel. But put him in a turban and that silly getup, and it was okay. Evidently, Indians from Asia were all right, if they wore costumes. I wondered idly how an American Indian, a native American, would be received. He'd probably be okay if he wore feathers and leathers.

No sooner had the door of 278 West 113th Street closed behind us than Manfred the Great spoke up.

"You two listen to me," he said. "Sargeant can say what he wants, but from here on in, you're working for me. Got it?"

"Gotcha, Manfred," Matty said.

"Very well," he said, "so long as we understand each other." Then he held out his hand. "I'll take the cash that Sargeant advanced you."

"Whaat?" we both said.

"For your expenses and for training you to be my assistants," he said.

Matty was cool. He knew he couldn't tick off Manfred. We needed him to get to San Francisco. Instead of telling the magician to take a flying jump for himself, Matty smiled innocently and said, "That's swell with me, Manfred. But Mr. Sargeant didn't say a word about us giving you money. I probably understood him wrong. Let's just go back and get it cleared up...."

"Uh...forget it," Manfred said. "We have a streetcar to catch. And don't forget, Owen, when we get to the hotel, you are Prince Rajat Singh. You're a magician from Bengal, India. Try to *look* professional."

"Your wish is my command, *sahib*," Matty said with a low bow.

We caught a streetcar on Broadway and 113th, and headed down to the hotel on Thirty-third Street. What a group we must have made: Fred Mann, known as Manfred the Great; Prince Rajat Singh, once Matty Owen, jazz drummer; and me. I didn't have a stage name. All I had was the paper suitcase, Manfred's parcel, and a five-dollar bill. I smiled. And Matty had thought *he* was going to be doing all the fetch and carry. Well, I thought, princes don't carry their own cardboard luggage, I guess....

7

Magic Is Hard Work

I was wrong about how much things would cost in 1906. Manfred took Matty and me to a men's store after we'd checked into the hotel. We both got suits, shirts, decent shoes, and overcoats. A hat for me (Matty didn't need one; he had his turbans) brought the whole bill to a bit over twenty-five dollars. Manfred charged it all to Houdini's bill. Looking good, we went with Manfred to the magic workshop Houdini had on Thirty-sixth Street, near Eighth Avenue.

Then the lessons from Manfred began. I learned the way some of the tricks I'd seen for years were really done. I had to know how, because to be even a magician's fetch-and-carry man, you have to know *what* to fetch and at the right time. Timing is everything in stage magic.

For instance, as Prince Rajat Singh, Matty had to walk up a ladder of razor-sharp swords. But I was the guy who had to set up the sword rack that became a ladder. The swords weren't really razor-sharp. In fact, you'd have a hard time cutting scrambled eggs with one of them. I learned how the Chinese linking rings worked. You've probably seen the gag—a series of metal rings that seem to pass through one another, yet can be connected to form patterns.

I learned how to "load" the dress suit that Manfred wore in the act. A magician's stage suit has more pockets than a crowd of kangaroos. In a very short time, Matty and I learned how some of the slickest illusions of all time were done. Naturally, becoming professional at this point, we were sworn to secrecy about how they were brought off. But I guess there's no harm in explaining a couple of them.

Manfred worked a gag (that's what tricks were called) we'd heard Sargeant mention earlier: Metamorphosis. I saw Doug Henning do it in the 1970s. I thought it was brand-new, but the gag has been around for years. As simply as possible, it's a quick switch.

Manfred is handcuffed by his assistant, in this case Matty, and sewn inside a big, black velvet sack by somebody from the audience. Then Manfred is put inside a trunk, which is later locked and wrapped in chains. Matty draws a curtain around the trunk and sticks his head out of the curtain.

Then Matty calls to the audience, "I'm going... I'm going...." He pulls his head behind the curtain and hollers, "I'm gone!" A second later, the curtain parts and instead of Matty, Manfred steps out! Next, Manfred opens the curtain and reveals the trunk, with all the locks and chains still intact. When the trunk is unlocked and opened, there's Matty, sewn inside the bag. The stitches are cut, and out pops Matty, with the handcuffs on his wrists! Marvelous, huh?

What the audience doesn't know is that the trunk is "gaffed." It's a trick trunk, and the end of it is hinged so it can swing inward. The fact that there are chains on it doesn't matter.

The sack that Manfred gets sewn into is no gag, but he has a small knife in one of his suit pockets. Soon as the trunk is closed, he gets rid of the handcuffs, which are rigged to open easy. Then he cuts open the bottom of the sack, pops the trick door in the trunk, and takes his place behind the curtain.

When Matty does the "going, going...gone!" bit, Manfred is already out of the trunk. When Manfred comes out from the curtain, all eyes are on him. In the next few seconds, Matty has to get inside the trunk and the sack and put on the handcuffs. It takes an awful lot of practice to do it fast enough. Most of the time, Matty was still putting on the handcuffs inside the sack when Manfred was opening the trunk.

Oh, yeah. About the sack. Doesn't anybody notice that the bottom is cut? Nope. They're too busy making sure the stitches at the *top* of the sack are intact. And when Matty stands up in the trunk, he's standing on the bottom of the bag, keeping it together!

It sounds easy when you know how it works. But Matty had a devil of a time getting in and out fast enough. Lots of times, he scraped his hands or face, getting through the trick door in the end of the trunk. The handcuffs, of course, were a gag. A funny thing about handcuffs. Even when they're not rigged, they're easy to get out of. I felt like a dummy to have been locked up in Judge Minton's chicken coop. I could have shed those cuffs in a flash. All you need is a simple steel pick.

Armed with a flat piece of steel, no bigger than a penknife blade, and a wire pick, Matty and I found out we could open almost any lock made in 1906. After we'd get done practicing all day, we'd goof around opening the doors to our rooms at the hotel without any keys. I'll tell you, it's a good thing magicians are honest. Even a fair magician could make a fortune as a burglar.

Not that I ever thought of becoming a burglar, but I made sure from that week on that I always had a wire pick and a flat piece of steel inside the lapel of my overcoat. I opened the seam and made two little pockets to keep them in. Matty did, too. We got the idea from all the secret pockets in Manfred's suit.

Outside of the endless practice sessions at the workshop, we didn't see too much of Manfred. Which was just as well. He wasn't what you'd call swift company to be with. Each chance he got, he'd badmouth Houdini.

I didn't know what to make of Manfred, except that he was a very unhappy man. Here, Houdini had set him up in the magic biz, and all he could do was to be jealous of his cousin-in-law's success.

I can't say I cared too much for Manfred's pals, either. One night, after rehearsals, Matty and I were going up to the Victoria to catch Houdini. Manfred was in the lobby, talking with this guy who could have posed for King Kong's double. As we passed by them, we both said hi. Manfred didn't introduce us. I heard the gorilla say to Manfred, "Who's the kid and the flashy nigger?"

"A couple of punks Houdini made me hire," Manfred told him.

"Do they know anything?" the ape asked.

"They don't know beans from buttons," Manfred answered. I made a mental note to fill Manfred's pockets with beans some night.

It was quite a change this night going to the Victoria, considering the lines that discouraged us days before. We went straight through the crowds to the Stage Door. Houdini had left our names with the doorman.

We watched the show from the wings, and Houdini was wowing the audience. He got eight curtain calls, and had to beg off. After a few minutes' wait, we were admitted to the Great Magician's dressing room.

"Come in, boys," he said, with that terrific smile of his. "How's it going with Manfred?"

Matty and I looked at each other. Without saying a word, it was decided between us not to bother Houdini with our problems. I nodded, and Matty said, "Just great, Houdini...real great." Houdini burst out laughing.

"Relax, boys," he said. "Nobody gets along with Manfred. But I appreciate your loyalty. You didn't say anything against him. Didn't say anything for him, either. That's hard to do.

"But let's not talk about Fred Mann. I'm glad you two showed up. I've been busy as a one-armed paperhanger with a broken belt. I have a European tour coming up, and I'll be *woiking* the Southern circuit before I leave for England. I'll be breaking in the milk can escape on this trip."

"Then you've got it working already?" I asked.

"I had the gag *woiked* out in my mind, fast as you described it," Houdini said. "What took the time was having my *woikshop* build it. I tell you, it's going to knock the show business on its ear, boys! It's a simple gag. Simple ones are the best and safest. And I'm going to be *woiking* on the Chinese water cell thing, soon as I get back from Europe. So I guess this is good-bye for us. You'll be leaving in a day or so, right?"

"That's right," Matty said. "First stop: Buffalo."

"Then, if I'm right about your gate to the future being in San Francisco, we won't ever see each other again," Houdini said, and extended his hand. We shook hands all around.

At the door I tried to thank him again for his help. He stopped me with a wave of his hand.

"I don't want to hear any more," he said. "And don't you go telling anyone, either."

"Not tell the world what a great guy you are?" asked Matty.

"When you do a *mitzvah*," Houdini said, wagging a finger, "you don't need to take a brass band with you. Now get out of here. I got another show to do!"

We made our way back to the Belvedere. On the street car, going to the hotel, Matty commented: "Gee, what a swell guy." I put a finger to my lips, and we both nodded. Houdini didn't need a brass band. The world would remember him as a swell guy, and the greatest stage magician who ever lived. Maybe that was reward enough.

Then, before we knew it, rehearsals were over with. It was time to get on the road, and off to San Francisco. By way of Buffalo, Cleveland, Toledo, Detroit, Chicago, and who-knew-where.

8

Shuffle Off to Buffalo

Buffalo, New York, in February was cold as a math teacher's kiss. When we got off at the railroad station, the wind cut right through our new overcoats and down to the bone. I was glad that this would be one of Manfred's better bookings. It meant we would stay at a large hotel. Big places had big heating plants. So did big theaters, and the Lafayette was large. It was also the first time I was to see a full program of vaudeville.

What a show those people put on! There were ten acts on the program, and we did three shows a day, starting in the morning. I hadn't expected many people for the morning show, but I was dead wrong. Mostly, the audience was little kids. I found out later that working mothers would often drop their kids off at the theater, buying them the cheapest seats. In the case of the Lafayette, it cost fifteen cents. When you think about it, where could you get a baby-sitter for a day, that cheap?

The show started with the band playing some of the songs popular in 1906, while people filed into the theater. Then the first act went on. These acts that opened the show were called dumb acts. Not because the people in

70

them weren't bright, but because they never spoke a word onstage. Smart thinking, as the audience was still coming in while the first act was on.

But those show people really worked hard. In Buffalo, the opening act was called Franklin & Company. Franklin was an acrobat, and the & Company was his entire family. Manfred called them a rizzly act. If you've never seen one, a rizzly act has the whole company come onstage in tights and then set up these thingies that look like those TV chairs that sit on the floor.

Two of the acrobats then lie down on the stage with their backs braced by the TV-chair gadgets and with their legs up in the air. They then proceed to balance large balls on the bottoms of their feet and toss them back and forth. After they do the ball toss, they begin tossing other members of the act from one place to another.

Next came a guy who worked with a trained chimpanzee. The act was called Johnson and Friend. The big funny of the act came when the trainer explained that it was the *monkey* who was named Johnson.

Then came a music act, a quartet. They sang popular songs and made some horrendously bad jokes in between. They were followed by a spot called an olio. This was a scene from a Shakespeare play as enacted by the Edmund Lance Players. Lance was an ex-Shakespearean actor who was no longer popular. I later found out it was because he couldn't stay sober. He did the soliloquy from *Hamlet* and then, with a girl young enough to be his daughter, did the balcony scene from *Romeo and Juliet*.

By the time the eighth act went on, I was numb from watching. Manfred had star billing in Buffalo, so his act was the big act. I learned it went on next to last and didn't close the show. The theater always put a pretty shabby act on last. This was so the customers would leave and there'd be room for more people.

Matty was already in his Prince Rajat Singh outfit and came to stand next to me in the wings to watch the eighth act. It was a song-and-dance act named Murphy and Francis. The two guys were entering from our side and stood alongside us as they waited to go on. Matty and I did a turn. Murphy and Francis were wearing blackface makeup. The heavyset one, Murphy, looked at Matty in his Rajat Singh outfit and gave him a smile.

"How's tricks, brother?" he said.

Matty looked at the man in stony silence. Then he looked closer. "You're really bla...er, colored!" he said in amazement.

"What'd you expect, Chinamen?" said the thin one, then they were out on stage, doing a dance together. Matty watched them in open-mouthed surprise.

"Richie," he whispered to me as the dance went on, "those guys are black. But they're wearing blackface makeup."

"What of it?" I asked.

"I didn't even know there were black acts in vaudeville."

"I never saw a rizzly act until today," I answered, "so now I know. What's the big deal?"

"But this is great," Matty said, all excited. "I have someone to talk to."

"Gee, thanks, pal," I said sarcastically, but I have to admit, my feelings were hurt. Matty saw the look on my face.

"I'm sorry, Richie," he said. "That didn't come out the way I meant it. But think. Since we've been back in time, we've been social with exactly two black people: Abner Pew and Mrs. Gilchrist. I don't count your girlfriend in 1942.

She was with you. But we'll be working a week with Murphy and Francis. I can talk to them. You *do* understand, don't you?"

"Sure, sure," I said, still miffed. "I wonder where they're staying in Buffalo? I bet they won't be..."

"Shhh!" Matty said. "They're going to sing a song now. I don't want to miss this."

Murphy and Francis sang a tune, all right. It was their opening number, titled "Though We're Irish by Name, We're Coons by Nature." They went on to sing another called "If the Man in the Moon Was a Coon, What Would You Do?" The lyrics continued: "There'd be no more strolling through the park at night / No more singing 'bout the pale moonlight. If the Man in the Moon was a coon, what would you do?"

They did a bunch of gags that would make any black person of the 1970s cringe, then reach for a phone to call the NAACP. The look on Matty's face had to be seen to be believed.

Murphy and Francis got off to thunderous applause. The Buffalo audience, it seemed, didn't share Matty's distaste for their material. As the two black men exited and passed us, the heavyset one said to Matty, "Great audience, brother. You'll knock 'em dead!"

Matty was so shook up he almost missed the opening music and his cue to go onstage to assist Manfred. We finished the first day's shows with Matty still mumbling to himself.

I was packing up Manfred's stuff and preparing it for the next day's shows with Matty when the heavyset partner of Murphy and Francis came over to us. He was wearing street clothes, not the raggedy costume he wore onstage.

To my surprise, he was quite light-skinned, about the same color as Matty.

"Hey there, Prince," the heavy man called out. "I saw your turn. You're pretty good."

Matty straightened up from adjusting the metamorphosis trunk and looked at the man. "Thank you," he said shortly and went back to what he was doing.

"Say, don't be that way," the man said. "We haven't met, though, have we? I'm Murphy. I was telling Francis while you were on: Why don't we have a cup of coffee with the Prince after the show?" He paused and looked Matty straight in the eye. "You *do* speak English, don't you, Prince?"

"Of course I speak English," Matty said, almost rudely. "I'm an American."

Murphy laughed. "I knew it, I knew it! I said to Francis, 'If that boy is from India, I'll eat the Taj Mahal.' What part of the country you from, Prince?"

"My name is Owen, Matthew Owen," Matty said sharply to Murphy. "Don't call me Prince. I feel like a dog."

"Funny line, funny line," Murphy said, smiling. "Well, how's about it? Feel like a cup of coffee with me and Francis?"

I saw the look on Matty's face. I knew how he felt about this man's act. But as I looked at Murphy's face, so kind and wanting to be so friendly, I answered for both of us.

"Sure we do, in a few minutes. We have to set up for tomorrow's show. Where are you going to have coffee?"

"There's a colored restaurant not far from here," Murphy said. "Charlie Ben's on Edward Street. You're both welcome. You can walk it from here, but it's so cold, you ought to take a cab."

"Are you cabbing?" I asked. "We could split the fare if you can wait a few minutes."

Murphy laughed loud and long. "Sonny, of course we're walking. You think a colored boy can just hail a cab in downtown Buffalo? Maybe the Prince here can. He got that disturbin' turban on his head. But us regular folks take Shank's mare."

I guessed that by Shank's mare he meant walking. I'd heard a lot of 1900s slang in the theater, and half of what was said missed me. "We'll all walk together, then," I said. Then I asked Matty, "You done yet, *Prince?*"

"Just about," Matty said in an annoyed tone.

"Okay, then," Murphy said. "We'll meet you at the stage door."

"What did you do that for?" Matty demanded angrily, once Murphy had left. "I don't want to go anywhere with those guys."

"Hey, pal," I replied, "I thought you wanted to talk to someone black for a change."

"After what they did on the stage out there? I'd sooner have a drink with the KKK!"

"Come on, man," I said, "he was being friendly. What are you, some kind of snob?"

"Maybe I am, Richie," Matty said, passing a hand over his face. "I still can't get over that tune...that *coon* song." He made it sound like a dirty word, which it is, I suppose. "It's one thing to hear the words from white people. I can understand where they're coming from in 1906. But to hear my own kind, doing it on a stage to make the white man laugh...It sickens me, Richie, it makes me want to puke."

"Maybe *they* don't think it's too swift, either, Matty," I

said. "Maybe it's just a pose. Murphy sure didn't talk the same offstage as he did onstage. You know, I think you're prejudiced."

"I'm *what?*"

"You heard me. You judged those two guys by what they did in their act. In our act, you're Prince Rajat Singh. I don't see you sitting on rugs and salaaming when you're off, though."

So we joined Murphy and Francis for coffee at Charlie Ben's. We didn't talk much on the walk over. It was so bitterly cold, we had to wrap our faces against the icy blast of the February wind. Murphy and Francis both had mufflers, which they kept over their faces. Matty and I had to make do with our overcoat lapels. Even so, when we got inside the little restaurant, on a side street, Matty's mustache was caked with white ice.

Charlie Ben's was a one-room place with a half-dozen tables and a long bar that ran the length of the room. Behind the bar, and on the walls in the dining room, were posters for and photographs of all the black acts that played Buffalo. It seems that Charlie Ben's was the black show-business hangout in that city.

Murphy had a full breakfast. His partner, like Matty and me, only ordered coffee. As soon as we sat down and thawed out, we introduced ourselves.

"I was surprised to see colored men onstage," I told Francis, the thin fellow. "When I saw you two in blackface makeup, I thought you were white men at first."

"You can't be in the business very long, Richie," Francis said. "There are many Negro acts in vaudeville." He had a rich, well-modulated voice. His way of speech indicated a good education.

"How come we've never seen any in the ads?" I asked.

"Depends on where you look," Murphy said. "I'd say there are over a hundred colored acts. Look at all the pictures on the walls here." He leaned back in his chair and began to point out individual photographs. "Over there, you got Walker and Williams. Very big act in the East. And that's Avery and Hart. They copy Walker and Williams a lot. Then there's the Holiday Sisters, Grace Holiday and Ada Overton...."

"Do they all do those coon acts?" Matty asked pointedly.

"Some do; some don't," Francis put in easily. "There's two light-skinned fellas...Cooper and Robinson. They do a *Jewish* dialect act."

"You gotta be joking," I said. "That act, I want to see."

"A lot of people do, Richie," Murphy said. "They're stars."

"But what have you got against coon acts, Matty?" Francis asked.

Matty took a deep breath. I knew he couldn't tell these guys who and what we really were. But I also knew he was deeply troubled about what he'd seen Murphy and Francis do onstage at the Lafayette.

"It's the whole idea of acting stupid and shuffling your feet for the white man to laugh at," Matty said. "You're giving the public a picture of our race as stupid, shiftless, and comical."

"Whoa, hold on, Matty," Francis said quickly. "Murph and I didn't invent that picture. It started with the white man's minstrel shows. Besides, I don't think that people really believe the characters we play. No more than they think all Jews are like the Hebe acts they see. My booking agent is Jewish, and he went to New York University. If it comes to that, I'm a graduate of Fisk."

"Then how can you do what you do?" Matty asked.

"You walked here with us, Matty," Murphy answered for Francis. "Did you notice how cold it was on the street?"

"Sure, I did."

"Well that's just where I would be if it wasn't for the show business. And where do you think Francis, with his diploma, would be? I'll tell you. Maybe teaching at a colored school someplace. If he was *lucky*.

"Me, I never got past sixth grade. Francis has been my college education. And look at the two of us...how we dress. This is a fifty-dollar suit I'm wearing. How long do you think it'd take me to save fifty bucks shining shoes or sweeping up white folks' garbage? There's worse things for the soul than doing a coon act, Matty!" He stopped and smiled. "I'm starting to sound like a preacher here. But I tell you, vaudeville is one of the few places in this country where a man is a man, no matter what color."

"Murph is right," Francis put in. "Vaudeville doesn't draw color lines. Show folk are the best people you'll ever meet. Sure, maybe some of them from the Deep South are hard to get along with. But they don't last long."

"What do you mean?" I asked.

"If your insides are filled with hate, there's no way you can fool an audience about it," Francis said. "All that meanness shows, and the people feel it. Like Walter Kelly, he bills himself as the Virginia Judge. Does comedy monologues."

"Yeah," Murphy said. "Francis, tell him what Hammerstein did to Walter Kelly when he said he wouldn't work on the same stage with Walker and Williams."

"Fired Kelly," Francis said, "and kept Walker and Williams! Now, Matty, tell me about show folks."

Francis finished his coffee and took a watch from his vest pocket. "It's getting late, men," he said. "Murph and I have a long walk ahead of us."

"Are you staying far from here?" I asked.

"We're at the Royal Hotel."

"That's where we are," I said. "We can walk together."

"Do you mind if I finish my breakfast first?" Murphy asked. "All this talking, I didn't get to eat!"

When we got back to the Royal, there was a surprise. As we entered the lobby, I glanced into the bar. Sitting at a table was Manfred, and he was with the same gorilla type I'd seen in New York. I mentioned it to Matty.

"Big deal," Matty said lightly. "Maybe the guy's a fan of Manfred's and follows him around. Kind of a turn-of-the-century groupie."

"Very funny," I replied. "I tell you I don't trust the looks of that guy."

"If it comes to that, do you trust Manfred?"

"Of course not."

"Then why should his pals be any nicer than he is? Come on, Richie. I'm worn out. Let's hit the sack."

We finished up in Buffalo to good reviews in the papers. I read the closing reviews on the train headed for Cleveland, our next booking. I'd just got done reading our notices when an item on the facing page caught my eye.

BANK OFFICIALS MYSTIFIED, POLICE ARE BAFFLED!

This morning, when the president of the Third National Bank, John Garrison, opened the locked safe for the day's business, he found the entire contents of fifty thousand dollars unaccountably missing.

Police investigators determined that the vault door

had not been tampered with or jimmied in any way. Only Garrison and Vice-President E. G. Gude have keys to the safe. Both men had attended a banquet the evening before the loss, and their whereabouts are well documented. They were in the company of our own Chief of Police Burns.

Chief Burns would not comment or venture an opinion as to how the vault was opened and looted. Only that he has "several clues."

I nudged Matty, who was sitting next to me, dozing. "Matty," I said, "look at this item in the paper."

He scanned the article and sat bolt upright in his seat. We both looked at each other, then up ahead in the car, where Manfred sat, his hat over his eyes.

"Do you think...?" I began.

"I wouldn't put anything past Manfred where money is concerned," Matty said. "But a safecracker? I don't know, Richie. It could be a coincidence."

"Sure, sure. And pigs have wings."

I got up and walked to the men's room at the back of the car. As I did, I glanced at the platform between our coach and the one behind us. Standing on the narrow space, smoking a cigar and watching the snow-covered countryside slide by, was the apeman pal of Manfred's!

9

That Toddlin' Town

It was just as well we had a good time in Buffalo. It was our last for some time. I hadn't realized when the tour was described to me, how much hard work was involved. We only worked six days, but our days off weren't really that. We had to get to the next city we played, and that was almost always a day's travel.

There was little rest on our travel days, either. Before we could even get on the train, Manfred's props had to be carefully packed in their custom crates and then put aboard. As it was, the equipment traveled better than we did. We all rode on what they called day coach, which was another laugh. We never took the train except at night. We didn't have sleeper cars. We slept sitting up in the coaches.

Buffalo was also the last of the hotels until we got to Chicago. For Cleveland and Detroit, we stayed at theatrical boarding houses. Maybe we could have stopped at hotels, but Manfred's famous cheapness showed up after Buffalo. Boarding houses were where most of the vaudeville performers, big time and small, stayed. In fact, in vaudeville, they were big business.

The reasons boarding houses were so popular were three:

for a dollar a day, you got a bedroom, the john down the hall, and your meals. You could even get your shirts done for a dime each. Considering Matty and I had only two shirts apiece, that came in handy. No-iron or drip-dry shirts were still years from then. So was same-day-service dry cleaning. Matty was okay, because he had a costume he wore onstage. He could have his suit cleaned and wear his dumb Indian outfit. I had to wait until Matty's suit was clean, then borrow his while mine was done. But shirts were the problem. The first time we washed them ourselves, we realized we didn't have an iron. We both looked like a pile of wrinkled laundry until we found out about the service the boarding houses offered.

All the boarding houses were called Ma Something-or-Other's or Mother So-and-So's or Mom Whoozis's. It seems that mothers in show biz never died, they opened theatrical boarding houses. Some of the places were okay, but others were nightmares. Manfred just went for the cheapest he could find.

After a while, Matty and I began to pay attention to the little handwritten notes that performers would leave on the bulletin board. About how good or bad the local boarding houses were. You could see notes like: "Stay away from Mom Fisher's, unless you like bedbugs." "Ma Flannagan's: pork seven days a week, with pork for dessert." And more ominous: "Stay at Mother Smith's. Her son is the manager of the theater. If you don't, he'll send a bad report on your act to New York."

After a time, the places fell into patterns. The first day you checked in, they'd put out a good meal, usually chicken. Then, on the day you were due to leave, they did it again. In between, the meals were pretty shabby. The idea was,

I guess, to welcome you with a good dinner and send you off the same way. Hoping you'd forget the garbage they served the rest of the time. But some silly things did go on at those places.

Matty and I usually shared a room. In Cleveland, we were sure that the act in the room next to us was going to die of pneumonia. We hardly slept because he kept coughing all night long. I mean, you'd have thought the guy was at death's door. Until we found out he worked with a trained seal. It wasn't him coughing; it was the seal making noise.

It was a good thing to be on the top floor of the places. If you weren't, it'd be your luck to be under a dance troupe that practiced at night after the show. This isn't to say there weren't good times. I liked the times in the parlors best. In 1906, a living room was called a parlor. The boarding houses had a piano there, and very often after the show, or between shows, the other acts would try out new tunes or routines on their fellow vaudevillians.

Chicago was a disaster. Manfred was the second magician in a row to work the theater, and Griffith the Magnificent, the guy who preceded us, had almost the same act as Manfred did. There being no copyright laws on acts, many times performers would steal any gimmick that came their way. Manfred went into the ground in Chicago. Hard. And for the first time, the drinking began.

I had the props all set up for the second day's show: a matinee. But fifteen minutes before Manfred was due onstage, he was still in his dressing room. The stage manager told me to go get him or we'd be canceled. Serious stuff. I knocked on his dressing-room door.

There was no answer, so I let myself in. Manfred was

sitting or almost sitting, in a chair in front of his dressing-table mirror. He was so drunk, he could barely move.

"Ten minutes, Manfred," I told him. "You're on in ten minutes."

He looked at me blearily and said, "Richie! My old pal. What are you doing here?"

Oh, great, I thought. "You have to go on, Manfred," I said. "It's time! The manager's getting real mad, too."

"Hell with him," Manfred mumbled. "With all of them. With Chicago and Griffith the Magnuff...Migneff..." He waved a drunken hand. "Whatever his name is..."

With this, Manfred slid off his chair and onto the floor. His eyes closed and he began to snore like a buzzsaw in heat. Matty came into the room and said, "Five minutes..." then trailed off when he saw Manfred the Great on the floor. "Oh, no!" he said.

"Oh, *yes,*" said I.

"What are we going to do?" Matty asked. "The stage manager is having kittens out there!"

"What's this *we* stuff, keemosabe?" I said. "It's all on Manfred. We're ready to go on."

"Yeah, but if they cancel Manfred, we get canceled, too. We promised Houdini we'd work our way cross-country. And after all, the show must go on!"

"I've been hearing that phrase all my life," I said. "Tell me, *why* must the show go on?"

"Because if it doesn't, we don't get paid, that's why. And even with our tickets, it's a long railroad trip to San Francisco. How do we eat?"

"You're right," I said. "The show must go on. Give me a hand with Manfred. Let's see if we can get him on his feet."

It was no good. He was like a stuffed doll that was worn out. Stand him up, and he flowed onto the floor again. It was getting later and later. Matty let go of Manfred's shoulders, and his head hit the dressing room floor with a thump. He started peeling Manfred's stage suit off the inert body.

"What are you doing?" I cried. "Keep trying. We have to get him onstage!"

"He *is* going onstage," Matty said, tugging at Manfred's pants. "You're going to be Manfred the Great!"

"*You're* going to be put away in a rubber room!" I hollered. "How can I be Manfred?"

"You know the whole routine. You know how everything works," Matty said. "You're about Manfred's size; the suit fits."

"You're about Manfred's size, too. Why not you?"

"Get real. Manfred talks onstage; I don't. If I went out there in his suit, they'd expect me to sing coon songs!"

There came a furious pounding on the door and the stage manager's voice hollered, "Manfred, get your tail out here! I already put the chaser on. If you're not ready in twelve minutes, you're canceled!"

"Right out, my man," I hollered back in what might have sounded like Manfred's voice. I scrambled into Manfred's suit and checked all the hidden pockets in his tailcoat and trousers.

Ten minutes later, I was standing in the wings, keeping my back to the stage manager, with Matty blocking his view, too. If he saw it was me, the manager would have canceled us on the spot. As it was, the last act, or "chaser" as he'd called it, had gone on, and a lot of the audience was leaving. I saw why. It was a trained dog act. Mangy.

The band started to play our music, and the emcee intoned: "Ladies and Gentlemen. The Rialto is proud to present, for your mystification and delight, that master of legerdemain, oracle of the occult...Manfred the Great!" There was a spattering of applause, and with my knees knocking like castanets, I stepped out on the stage.

Now, I knew the routine backward and forward. I knew how each trick was done. It was my job to set it up each show. But there's a world of difference between knowing and doing in front of six hundred people.

The first stunt was the Chinese linking rings. I got through it almost all the way, until I was supposed to take them apart. I couldn't budge them! I got them all fanned out and interlocked, but when it came time to separate them, my hands turned to stone. I tugged and pulled, made the necessary moves, and still no good.

The audience was silent at first, then they began to laugh. "Well, they're supposed to come apart," I said lamely. The house roared. Next, I was to do a venerable magic gag: pull a rabbit out of a hat. It wasn't a real bunny, just a stuffed doll. That was part of the gag. When the audience would protest that it wasn't a real rabbit, I'd wave my hand and turn it into a bouquet of flowers.

The rabbit doll contained the folding bouquet, of course. They weren't real flowers, either. They were made of silk, and could be folded up on a steel-sprung "stem" to look almost real. I announced that I was going to pull a rabbit out of the hat, and stuck my hand inside the hat, which was on a magic tray on a tripod. The tray had a false bottom that the flowers and rabbit doll were taken from. The hat had a top that folded back so you could do it.

"*Voilà!*" I cried taking out my hand. "A rabbit!" Except I had a bouquet of flowers in my hand. The audience wouldn't stop laughing, even when I tried again. This time, I came up with a pitcher of water. It was a phony pitcher they use onstage. It had a fluid inside, but it also had a glass inner cover, so it wouldn't spill. I set the pitcher down on the tray too quickly. It fell off, and instead of spilling its contents, it bounced!

When Prince Rajat Singh was introduced, the audience was laughing so loud, you could hardly hear my words. I set up the ladder of swords the way I should have. I showed the swords, one at a time, demonstrating how they'd cut right through a sheet of newspaper. Actually, the newspaper strips were precut. As I passed the blade "through" them, I'd let go of the strips, and they'd float to the ground.

Once I had all the swords on the rack, stage center, so they formed a ladder, I'd "hypnotize" the prince. He was supposed to walk up the "ladder of steel" in his bare feet, then turn around and descend it. I would take a sword and again "cut" a paper strip to show how sharp the blade was.

Matty got to the top of the sword ladder just swell. The crowd even stopped laughing. It's an effective gag. What sort of spoiled it was that the prince lost his balance as he turned around to come back down. Matty teetered back and forth, while the audience went *ooooh*, then bounced down each of the "razor-sharp" swords on his yellow, satin-clad buns! When he got up, without even a snag in his pants, the house was hysterical.

"Ladies and gentlemen," I announced over the laughter, "I will now produce, from thin air, no less than fifty silk handkerchiefs!"

I knew I could do this stunt. I went over to the magic tray, and one by one, I pulled fifty silk handkerchiefs of different colors from the hat. No trouble. I also had no trouble making them vanish again, seemingly into my fist. Actually, they were all going into a special part of the suit. The crowd stopped laughing, and once in a while, I got a bit of applause. I was now ready for the big finish.

The end of the gag is impressive. Once you make all the silks vanish, you make them appear again from your fist, and they're all tied together. The last silk is in the shape of an American flag. Guaranteed to get applause in 1906, and also get you offstage to a big hand. The silks are really different ones, all tied to begin with. They're wrapped around your waist and then run down your sleeve, so you can make them "appear" from your fist.

As the music played, I began unreeling the silks. It went great. As the pile of silks on the stage grew longer and longer, the house clapped more and more. Finally, the red, white, and blue silk was due to "appear," but the string of silks was stuck someplace around my waist. We'd put the magic suit on me so fast, it must have got tangled somehow. I pulled hard. Nothing. The audience began to giggle. I pulled harder. Still nothing. The house was laughing louder now.

"This isn't easy to do, folks," I said as the sweat ran down my face.

"It's pretty hard to *watch,* too!" someone hollered from the balcony, and the people came unstuck laughing. I tugged frantically on the chain of silks, then felt something rip. I'd pulled it free!

"And now, for the patriotic climax!" I cried, pulling out the last silks. Sure enough, the red, white, and blue showed. Just before my pants fell down. Matty and I stopped the show, you might say.

We got eight curtain calls, and when we begged offstage, I nearly fainted when the stage manager came over to me and said, "That's the best show Manfred *never* gave! In my whole life, I haven't laughed so hard!"

"It wasn't our fault," I began, "Manfred was sick...."

"Manfred was dead drunk, and we all know it," the stage manager said.

"He'll be all right for the next show," Matty said. "We'll be okay with the regular act by then."

"Not on your tintype, you won't," the man said. "Manfred was dying with that act. For the rest of the booking, I want what I just saw! I never heard of a comedy magic act before. Didn't you hear the suckers? Congratulations, kids. You're a hit. I think I saw the vaudeville critic from the *Times* out there. He fell off his seat laughing."

Stunned, Matty and I accepted handshakes and pats on the back from the acts that had been watching in the wings, once they'd heard all the laughs. We made our way back to Manfred's dressing room like stars.

When we came into the room, Manfred was sitting up, holding his head in his hands and groaning softly. "Whatever you do," he whispered, "don't slam that door." He looked up and for the first time noticed he was in his long johns and I was wearing his suit. I was holding the pants up with one hand as he said, "What are you doing wearing my outfit? Are you nuts? I'll be ready to go on in a minute."

"You already went on, Manfred," Matty said with a grin. "You wowed 'em. Eight curtain calls." Then we told him.

10

Wee Willie and
the Cruncher

We were backstage in Manfred's dressing room. He was still monumentally hung over. It took awhile for it to sink in on him that we'd done his act, and been a great success.

"They loved it?" he moaned.

"Had to beg off," Matty said.

"And the stage manager wants the same act, from now on," I added. I told him what he had said.

"I'm ruined in the business!" Manfred cried, then grabbed his aching head. "Ahh, what difference does it make?" he added. "I'm a dead man anyhow."

"Come on, Manfred," I said, "nobody ever died of a hangover."

"That's not what I'm talking about. There's two guys coming to the theater after the last show. They're after me. They're gonna kill me!"

"What are you talking about?" I demanded.

"You saw one of them," Manfred said. "Cruncher Fitzgerald. They call him that because he likes to break people's bones before he cuts their throats."

"You mean that big guy I saw in New York and Buffalo?"

"That's the one. His partner stayed out of sight. Wee Willie Ryan. He's a box man...a safecracker."

"They call him that because he's small?" Matty asked.

"Nahh, it's a nickname. He's bigger than Fitzgerald."

"Oh, swell," Matty said. "Why are these guys after you? Is it something to do with that bank robbery in Buffalo? Tell the truth, Manfred. We can't help you unless we know what's going on!"

Manfred raised his head and looked at us with red-rimmed eyes. "You mean you'll help me?" he asked piteously. "What did I ever do for you?"

"Nothing," Matty said, "and we ought to leave you to those gorillas. But we owe a lot to Houdini. And he says he owes you. In our book, that's the same thing."

Matty didn't mention that without Manfred's act, we'd have a devil of a time trying to reach San Francisco. Manfred looked grateful, like a stray dog that gets a surprise handout. I was going to say something, but Matty pressed on.

"It is about that Buffalo job, isn't it?" he asked.

"Yeah," Manfred admitted. "I wasn't part of it, though. See, I owe a lot of money to some bookies in New York. The ponies ain't been good to me lately. Wee Willie and the Cruncher bought my I.O.U.'s from the bookies. So I owe them, instead. But they didn't want money. Not any money I had, at least."

"Let me guess," I said. "They just had you open the doors to the bank, and the safe inside, right?"

"I never did that!" Manfred replied hotly. "I only agreed to teach Wee Willie how to open safes without using soup...nitroglycerine. I had a set of picks made for him. I had no idea they were going to pull that bank job in Buffalo."

"What'd you think they were going to do with the picks?" Matty asked pointedly. "Start an act in vaudeville?"

"I never thought they'd do anything in a town while I was working there," Manfred said softly. "When they showed me the fifty grand and told me we were square on my I.O.U.'s, I nearly died. I *shoulda* died, right there. But no, I had to get cute."

"What do you mean, cute?" I asked.

"I knew that soon as the cops started thinking, they'd put two and two together. That to open the bank and the safe required somebody like me. I mean, who else could have done it?"

I had to smile. Even in fear for his life, Manfred's ego was still bigger than his fright. "Matty or I could have done it, Manfred," I said.

"The cops would have arrested *all* of us," Manfred said.

"Oh, great," Matty moaned. "Just what we need. More cops after us!"

"Are you guys on the lam?" Manfred asked. "Is that why Houdini had me hire you?"

"Never mind us," Matty put in. "Nobody's chasing us. We're talking about you. And if these two crooks got their loot, why are they after you? Why do they want to kill you?"

"I told you. I got cute. I figured that if I somehow got the money back to the bank, I'd be okay. I knew where Cruncher and Wee Willie were hiding out. I waited until they were out casing a new job, here in Chicago...."

"Another one!" I hollered. "We have to stop them!"

"Will you let me finish?" Manfred cried. "I went to their place, slipped the lock, found their cash, and left. But I think the desk clerk at their fleabag hotel spotted me." He stroked his beard, the ham. "I'm a distinguished-looking man, you know. Anyway, I wrapped up the satchel with the cash in it; there was some already spent. I sent what was left to that bank in Buffalo, along with a note saying Wee Willie and Cruncher did the job. I thought the cops would have picked them up by now, but they haven't."

"So now they're after you for revenge," I said. "Do you know that for sure?"

Manfred nodded and reached over to his dressing table. He picked up a piece of paper and handed it to me. "It was with the doorman," he explained. I read it quickly and handed it to Matty. It was written in a schoolboy's scrawl.

> Manfred,
> Nobody crosses us and lives. You do the job with us tonight, maybe you won't die. Be ready after the last show. Or else.
>
> You know who

"Now what am I gonna do?" Manfred said, bouncing back into his "poor me" routine.

"Don't panic, is the first thing," Matty said. "I think I have a plan to get us all out of this. But you have to pull yourself together, Manfred. We'll need you."

"Anything...anything at all," Manfred said. Then he looked at Matty and added, "I won't have to be close to Cruncher, will I?"

"No closer than a few feet," Matty said. Manfred moaned again. Then Matty sat down, and we worked out our plot.

We did the last show as scheduled. I went on in Manfred's place again. I had a bit of trouble making my pants fall down on cue, but the audience went crazy for the show.

Later on, when the performers had left the theater, and

just the doorman and watchman were left, Matty went and peeked out the stage door. I stood behind him and took a look. Cruncher and a man about his size were standing out in the alley, pacing up and down. I looked back to the wings, where Manfred was waiting, and gave him a wave.

He went over to the doorman. "My good fellow," he said to the old man, "I have some friends waiting in the alley. But I must rehearse my assistants some more. Would you give them this note?" He handed an envelope to the door-man. He also took out a dollar bill, big money in 1906. He gave it to the doorman and said, "We'll also need some coffee. Would you run over to the restaurant and bring some back?"

"Sure thing, Mr. Manfred," the old man said. "One large coffee, coming up."

"And keep the change, my good chap," Manfred added. "You needn't hurry back."

"Yes, *sir,* Mr. Manfred!" said the doorman with a big smile. He went out the door, and Matty and I saw him hand the note to the two crooks. They read it and headed right for the stage door.

"Here they come!" Matty whispered to Manfred, who was now standing in the middle of the stage. "Get ready!"

I hurried to the lighting board backstage and killed all the lights, except for one baby spotlight, which shone on Manfred. I kept my hand close to a big lever, alongside the lighting panel. Matty scurried back to where the various ropes and pullies used to raise and lower scenery were secured. Manfred stayed rooted to the spot, barely moving. Sheer terror, I suppose. I didn't blame him a bit.

The stage door swung open, and the crooks came in. "Manfred!" called out the Cruncher. "Where are you?"

"Out here, on the stage," he called back. "Come on out. There's nobody in the house but us. I sent the doorman for coffee."

The two thugs strode across the stage. I thought they were going to jump on Manfred immediately. I put my hand on the lever and hoped Matty was in place.

"Awright, Manfred," Cruncher said. "You got ten seconds to live, unless you talk fast." He reached into his coat pocket and took out a knife. Manfred turned pale green.

"Where's our loot?" Wee Willie asked. He was standing alongside Cruncher.

"I sent it back to Buffalo," Manfred said weakly.

"You what?" growled Cruncher, and sprang at Manfred! That's when I pulled the lever. The trapdoor opened perfectly, and Cruncher disappeared with a wild yell. Immediately afterward, Matty released his rope backstage. Two immense, hundred-pound sandbags came thundering down on top of Cruncher. There was only one small hitch. Wee Willie wasn't standing on the trapdoor when it let go. He almost fell in when one of the sandbags brushed him as it whizzed by, but he regained his balance.

I rushed toward him from behind, thinking to push him into the yawning trapdoor, but he turned. He pulled a knife out of his belt that made Cruncher's weapon look like a toothpick. Manfred stood by, paralyzed with fear, his mouth open wide. Totally useless.

Wee Willie backed up so he was between me and Manfred, his eyes darting from side to side. "You maybe got Cruncher," he snarled, "but I'm gonna get you two!"

The two of us stood there as the man began to close in, flicking the knife toward me, then Manfred. Suddenly, with a blood-curdling whoop, Matty burst through the curtains behind him. In his hand was one of the swords from the act. He swung viciously at Wee Willie, who backed up. Again, Matty swiped at Willie. The blade whistled past him, inches away from his face. Willie jumped back involuntarily and went straight down through the trapdoor. As he landed, I heard him give off an animal-like cry. I ran back to the lighting board and threw some switches. The stage was bathed in bright white and colored lights.

Matty walked over and peered down the gaping hole in the stage. I saw him give a little shudder. Manfred, freed of his stonelike terror, joined him. He suddenly put both hands over his mouth and, retching, he dashed for his dressing room. I went to where Matty was standing and took a look for myself. It wasn't pretty.

In the light cast from the stage overhead, I could make out the still figures of Cruncher and Wee Willie. Cruncher had landed badly, and his head wasn't visible under a hundred-pound sandbag. Wee Willie had evidently landed on his own knife blade, then rolled over. I looked down into his face, contorted in horrid surprise. I felt a wave of nausea.

"What a way to die," I said, half to myself.

"They would have killed us both, pal," Matty said, putting a hand on my shoulder. "I'm just glad that Wee Willie was scared by the *looks* of this sword. If I'd have hit him with it, all he would have got was bruises."

It may have been relief from my fear, but I had to laugh at what Matty said. He broke up, too. In a few seconds, we were both howling, more in hysteria than anything else.

The Chicago police were very understanding. Both crooks were wanted in a half-dozen states. Naturally, Manfred took credit for it all. He made headlines. *Comic*

Magician Foils Criminals! the papers said. Matty and I ducked the reporters, which didn't bother Manfred at all. By the time he got done embroidering the truth, you'd have thought Manfred was Dick Tracy and Superman all rolled into one.

And it did wonders for business. We were held over for two weeks in Chicago. Manfred didn't care anymore that people laughed at his act. He even added a few new touches of his own. Like in Metamorphosis, he pretended he couldn't get out of the box!

11

San Francisco!

It seemed that the Western tour went on forever. Boarding houses with rotten food, lumpy beds, and endless train rides all blurred together into the pattern of three shows a day.

The only cheering note was the change in Manfred after Chicago. Not that he wasn't his usual egotistic, overbearing self, but Matty and I noticed the difference. Manfred didn't mind being laughed at onstage. Because of his newspaper clippings as a fearless crime fighter in Chicago, he'd get asked for autographs wherever we went. Somehow, the idea that he was really someone offstage as well as on took the sting out of the ridicule given to the comedy magic act.

And I have to admit it was funnier with Manfred doing the shows. He looked so imposing and dignified that when things went wrong, it made audiences laugh harder. He not only kept adding new pieces of business to the act, but by the time we reached San Francisco, he'd convinced himself that the comedy idea was his to begin with!

Sargeant had been right about San Francisco. Even at the turn of the century, it was a bustling, international-flavored city. As we rode from the railroad station toward our hotel in the theater district, Manfred acted like a guided-tour person, pointing out this and that. He'd played the city before, but this was different. He was coming to town not as a Houdini imitator, but as a star in his own right.

"Look who's in town," Manfred said, pointing to a marquee. "Caruso!"

In fact, it seemed that everyone was in town on April 17. Caruso was singing with the whole Metropolitan Opera Company from New York. I saw a theater advertising John Barrymore in a play called *The Dictator*. I'd seen John Barrymore on Late Show movies as an old character actor. But the picture they had of him outside the theater showed he was a very handsome man when he was young.

"San Francisco is a great town," Manfred told us, "and we are going to enjoy it, boys. No Mother Murphy's three meals and a bluff. We are staying at the Hotel de France!"

The place was elegant, all right. We had a whole day before we were to open at the Orpheum Theater. It happened because we'd been held over in Denver, and San Francisco had a different schedule for when their acts started. It was a real luxury: a day off!

Even though Manfred got a raise in pay, he never did pass the profits on to us. We'd long since paid back the five bucks apiece Sargeant advanced us. We were now earning five bucks a week each. But Manfred did buy us a swell dinner at the hotel.

To give you an idea of what a real, high-class hotel put out for meals, the menu was: a complete dinner, with all the soup you could eat, fish with "French sauce," which was a whitish wine dressing, and very tasty, then a huge slab of roast beef, with a half-quart of red wine, if you wanted it, pie for dessert, and all the coffee you wanted afterward.

The whole dinner check came to about *fifteen cents* per meal! Manfred even bought a ten-cent cigar, which was brought to the table in a humidor. He gave the waiter a dollar bill for the meal and said airily: "Keep the change, my good fellow." The guy followed us to the door, bowing and scraping all the way. Filled with dinner, Matty and I headed for our room. Manfred stuck around in the lobby, hoping someone might recognize him and ask for an autograph.

"I can't believe it!" Matty cried. "A room with a bath!"

He flopped down on the nearest bed. "No lumps in the mattress, either," he chortled. "I've really felt like Rajat Singh in those boarding houses. It was like sleeping on beds of nails. But this is heaven, Richie, absolute heaven, I tell you!"

I had to agree. I also had to smile a little. Over the past ten weeks or so, Matty and I had really become part of the year 1906. In our own time, a bed like this wouldn't have caused Matty to raise an eyebrow, let alone run on about it. Me neither. The weeks of hard work and harder living made us appreciate little things. I knew that if I ever got back to 1976, I wouldn't feel the same.

"I can't believe it's all over," Matty said to me. "We're really here in San Francisco."

"It's far from over," I said. "We don't know for sure there's a future gate in Golden Gate Park. If it comes to that, we don't even know where the park is from here."

"You know, you're right," Matty said, sitting up. "We have to find out right away."

"Time enough tomorrow," I said. "I want to take a bath first."

"After me," Matty said, getting up and dashing toward the bathroom. I was already halfway there. I won the race and got first bath.

Sitting in a hot tub with the steam rising, I felt like an oil sheik. I ignored Matty's hurry-up pleas and wallowed in the suds. The towels were big, thick, and numerous. There were even a couple of terry cloth bathrobes laid out near the oversized towels. I put one on and left the bathroom.

"All yours, pal," I said as Matty entered, "and all the hot water you want."

"If this is a dream," he said, "don't wake me up."

As I heard the water thundering into the tub, I lay back on the bed and reflected on 1906. Now that we were doing well, it wasn't all that bad. Then I thought about stories I'd read in newspapers on the long train rides.

In this year, people died young. From things like small-pox, typhoid, diptheria, and polio. Except they called polio "infantile paralysis" back then. Diseases that almost don't exist today. Some folks would die of diseases that we cure now with a few dollars' worth of antibiotics.

Kids and women worked in factories six and seven days a week, for almost no pay. The forty-hour work week with Saturdays and Sundays off was a dream. No one retired from a job. There was no Social Security. Or labor unions. If you looked the wrong way at a boss one day, you could be canned for no reason. No, on thinking about it, 1906 wasn't all that swift.

Just then, Matty came out of the bathroom, wearing a

robe just like mine. "Why so glum, chum?" he asked. "I thought you'd be dancing around the room for joy. We're going home!"

"Maybe yes, maybe no. We won't know for sure until we get to Golden Gate Park. If the key guides us right, we'll be back in 1976. But we'll still be in San Francisco. We have to get to New York...to Branford."

"Oh, I get it," Matty said. "And if we return at the exact moment we left, we're missing persons until we turn up in Branford."

"You got it, smart prince," I said. "And regardless of how sure you are that the gate is here, if it isn't, we're maybe stuck for life in this year."

Matty sat down on the bed next to me. "Yeah, you're right," he said in a subdued tone. "Geez, Richie, I don't think I could cut it, living in this time. Sure, I can wear a turban and go anyplace. But spend the rest of my life posing as a phony Indian prince? No way. Or even worse, go through life like Murphy and Francis, saying 'Yassuh boss' and shuffling my feet? Brrrr! It gives me the creeps!

"I tell you, Richie, if the gate isn't here, I'll spend the rest of my life trying to find it. I'll never give up!"

"Okay, okay. But what are you going to do when you get back home, then?"

"Well, the first thing I'll do is patch things up with my dad. It was a stupid fight we had, and I was wrong. I had the world by the tail in 1976 and didn't appreciate it."

"So, you'll be going back to school?"

"Absolutely. But it may not be Juilliard."

"Not be a musician? That's the first I've heard of *that*."

"Oh, I'll never give up the drums, Rich. But I've learned too much from being here, and the other years we visited."

He laughed shortly. "I thought it was rough being black in 1976. Ha! I had my head screwed on backward.

"I never knew what my parents and grandparents went through. This trip through time has been an eye-opener, pal. I'll never feel the same way about my rights as a citizen again. The way I was raised, I never saw Harlem or a ghetto in my life. Except on TV, when they had a fire or a riot there.

"My idea of prejudice was some clown giving me a dirty look or maybe making a snotty remark. Thanks to my dad, I never went hungry, and I went where I pleased. I had my own *car*, Richie, and I never worked to pay for it!"

"That makes you a bad guy?" I asked. "Lots of kids, black kids too, have that."

"Yeah, but there's also lots of black kids who go to bed hungry. When I get back, I want to do something about it. I know what hungry is now, Richie. And I know what being treated like a nonperson feels like. I want to see those things wiped out in our time. Like we wiped out diseases that kill folks here in 1906. And a musician isn't in a position to do that. That's why I may not go to Juilliard."

"Matty Owen, the black activist?" I asked, raising my eyebrows. "Can this be the same silver-tongued con man I've come to know and respect?"

"Don't make fun, Richie. I'm serious."

"Whatever you say, sport," I said. But I was wondering what I'd do with *my* life if...when we got back home. I wasn't qualified for any college I knew of. Harry would still be chasing after girls my age, and Mom would still be a drunk. What was I going back to?

"Hey, Richie, don't go deadly on me," Matty said, seeing

my expression. "I'm still your pal, and always will be. We've been through a lot together." Then he smiled like the old Matty and said, "What do you say we get dressed and look around? I'll bet we can get a map of the city down in the lobby. We'll pinpoint Golden Gate Park, and we can go there first thing in the morning."

"Manfred's gonna be let out when we don't make the first show."

"Up his, the cheap so-and-so. We got our payday, finally. We have some coins, and San Francisco is a real wild town. Let's do it right for our last night here!"

I decided Matty was right. I shook off my blues and put on my suit. We each had more than four weeks' pay saved. During the Western tour, there'd been no place to spend our salaries. In most of the towns we played out West, *we* were the only action in town. When the show was over, all you could do for laughs was go to the barber shop and watch haircuts. Maybe go to a general store and try on work gloves. Dullsville.

We got our San Francisco maps in the lobby and did some exploring around the hotel area. It seemed that every other location on our street was a bar with music or gambling, or both. Matty discovered roulette, at a place called McGurk's.

Figuring that all we needed was cab fare to Golden Gate Park, about a dollar, he bet ten dollars that the next number on the wheel would be odd, not even. It was, and he had twenty bucks. He let it ride. He had won another twenty.

"Let's go," I whispered to him as he stood at the table. "We have plenty of money now."

"What for?" Matty said, his eyes watching the ball rolling.

"If we're leaving tomorrow morning, what'll we do with 1906 money in 1976? It's just a game, Richie. It has no meaning." He let the forty bucks ride on odd numbers. And won again.

I guess if you don't care whether you win or not, gambling is entertainment. Maybe it even changes your luck. Matty could do no wrong. He shifted bets from odd to even. Then from black to red. Inside of ninety minutes, Matty had won close to five hundred bucks. A small fortune! As he promised me, the first time he lost, he quit.

We cabbed back to the hotel, although it was just two blocks away. Matty paid the cabbie with a five-dollar bill and told him to keep the change.

"Thanks, er...*mister,*" the white cab driver said.

Matty turned to me with a grin. "See? That's all you need to be a *mister*: bucks!" He turned to the driver and said, "Would you be here tomorrow morning at eight? There's another five in it for you."

"If there's another five, I'll *wait* here until then," the cabbie said.

"Do you have a wife and family, cabbie?" Matty asked.

"Yeah. Four kids, mister."

"Here," he said, "take this money and go home. Spend some time with your family." He handed the driver another five. "But remember, be here at eight."

"Yes sir!" said the driver. He cracked his whip and was off down the street. Matty and I went inside the Hotel de France, and Matty stopped at the desk to pick up some writing paper and envelopes. "Who're you writing to?" I asked as we rode up to our floor.

"You'll see," he said with a smile.

Back in the room, he emptied his pockets of the money

he'd won and strewed the bills across his bed. "What a gag," he said. "We went through all those troubles and dangers just to get here. All because we didn't have the coins for the train ride. Now we're here, and leaving tomorrow, we've got bucks up the gazookis."

"The way you've been tossing it around, it's good we're leaving."

"There's more to come," Matty said, and busied himself with pen and paper.

The note was to Mrs. Gilchrist. I read it and kind of choked up.

> *Dear Mrs. Gilchrist,*
> *Please accept this money and do with it what you want.*
> *But please, save fifty cents of it. One day, two strangers*
> *in trouble will need your help. Give them the fifty cents.*
> *God bless you.*
>
> *A Friend*

"I don't know, Matty," I said. "You send her all that cash, she might quit her job with Judge Minton in Branford."

"You're not thinking, Richie. If she did that, she wouldn't have been there in 1912, when we were."

"Then did she give us the fifty cents because she was a nice lady, or because you had sent her the note with money?"

"What difference does it make? She's a wonderful lady regardless, isn't she?"

"Yeah, but I keep thinking of what Abner Pew told us. What we do in the past can affect the future. Maybe even our own time."

"But it *didn't*, don't you see? Otherwise, we wouldn't have got this far."

"Guess you're right," I said.

Matty went down the hall to drop the letter in the corridor mail chute. I was already in bed when he returned and flicked off the room lights.

I lay in the darkness for a few minutes, looking at nothing. "Matty. Are you asleep?" I asked.

"Not now, pal. What's on your mind?"

"I don't know. But I have this funny feeling. Like something's gonna happen."

"Go to sleep. Nothing's gonna happen tonight."

Which shows you just how wrong an Indian prince can be.

12

Shake, Rattle, and Roll

I was dreaming that I was back on a train. The steady rocking and rumbling kept waking me. Somehow, this was different. It was more like...I sat bolt upright in bed. It wasn't a dream. The whole room was moving!

"Matty!" I hollered.

"Over here!" he called. He was already out of bed.

"What's going on?" I cried over the noise.

"I don't know, but I'm getting out of here!" he replied, grabbing at his coat.

I didn't have to get out of bed. In a second, I was on my hands and knees on the floor, as it shook from side to side crazily. I managed to grab at my overcoat just as the whole side of the wall that faced the street fell away.

"Earthquake!" I hollered, with a swell grip on the obvious.

Matty, who had kept his feet, grabbed the collar of the robe I'd worn to bed and began dragging me toward the door of the room. I got to my feet, and we both struggled through the door. The corridor wasn't any better. The whole world was reeling and shifting. We were on the third floor of the hotel, and it was threatening to become the ground floor at any moment.

If you've never been in an earthquake, and I hope you never are, it's almost impossible to describe the feeling. I think what panics you most is the fact that things that aren't supposed to move, do. It's one thing when you're in a building. If you can get outside, as Matty and I did, before the whole building comes crashing down, you expect you'll be okay. The horror of it is that when you're on the street, the street is shaking and moving, too! The ground itself isn't supposed to move, you keep telling yourself.

I felt something hit my shoulder as Matty and I moved away from the collapsing Hotel de France. My own fault. I had turned and looked back. Just in time to see the entire face of the building come falling down, opening up like the front of a kid's dollhouse. A piece of it had hit me.

The street was shaking under our feet like a funhouse walkway, and the rumbling noise kept getting louder. We would have run, but there was no place to run. We took a few steps toward the middle of the street to avoid any more falling bricks. The incredibly deep rumbling grew louder, like thunder. A big crack showed in the middle of the street, and a section the size of a Greyhound bus just sort of fell in, like a pie crust collapsing. A jet of water about ten feet high shot straight up into the air.

"Hit the dirt, Richie!" Matty cried, falling to the ground and taking me with him. We both huddled close together. I threw my one item of clothing, my overcoat, on top of my head. I don't know why. Maybe I had the dumb idea it'd stop any falling debris. If you think about it, a lot of good a piece of cloth does when a chunk of building the size of a truck falls on you. But who was thinking? I was petrified.

All around us, as I peeked out from under my coat, huge chunks of building facades were still falling, and there was glass all over the place. And then, there was the constant noise. Not only the sound of big pieces of buildings falling and people screaming, but the incredible bass rumble of the ground itself moving.

Across the way, another building, a five-story brick structure, began to go. I heard its death scream. It's the sound that tortured steel and masonry make as they are stretched by the moving earth to a point where they can no longer hold together. That death scream is a sound I'll carry with me to the day I die.

Then, suddenly, it stopped. Just like somebody had thrown a switch, the earth stopped moving. Matty and I got to our feet and began taking inventory of our body parts. They all seemed to be where they should, and in working order.

"You've got a cut on your shoulder, Richie," Matty said. "I think we'd better find a doctor. It might need..."

It began again! Without another word, Matty and I threw ourselves back on the ground. I found myself praying: "Oh God, please make it stop. I can't stand any more!" Maybe my prayer was heard. After a few seconds, the shaking quit. Again, Matty and I got to our feet.

"An aftershock," Matty said. "That happens."

"How would you know?" I said, dusting myself off.

"I read about it," Matty said. "So did you. Don't you realize what happened?"

"I may be hurt, but I'm not stupid," I came back. "It was an earthquake."

"Yeah, but it was *the* earthquake!" Matty went on. "The worst ever. If we'd used our heads, we never would have come here. This is the Great San Francisco Earthquake! The worst in our history."

"I'll buy that," I said.

"I just hope it's over," I told Matty. "Do you remember reading how long it lasted?"

"No. But it seemed like it went on forever. That may have been the only aftershock...." He broke off speaking and said, "Listen, Richie. Listen."

There wasn't anything to listen to, but I knew what he meant. There was silence. An eerie, complete, unhealthy silence. A city of any size is never completely quiet. If you listen late at night, you can always hear something—a passing car, a train, a footstep. Someone getting up to go to work early; someone coming home late. A city is never totally silent.

As we stood there on the street, looking at the devastation, we could hear each other breathing. About a block away, something sizable fell to the ground. Probably a piece of a building that had just been hanging and finally let go. In the weird quiet, it sounded like an explosion. We almost hit the dirt again, thinking the quake might be starting anew.

At that moment, we smelled what we'd learned to be careful of in 1906. An odor that meant death to so many in the years before central heat in buildings: escaping gas! There was no doubt a street-sized gas main had been ruptured. The danger of fire and explosion was so heavy in the air, you could almost feel it, as well as smell it. I knew the slightest spark could set it all off.

From a distance, we began to hear sounds. The first

thing we heard were fire bells. Evidently, fires had already begun. Then, all around us, we began to hear people. Talking, shouting, and crying out in pain. We got to our feet again.

"How's the shoulder look, Matty?" I asked.

"Hard to tell with the lights all out," Matty said. The street lamps, naturally, were gone. "If it wasn't such a bright night, I couldn't see a thing....Richie, look at the sky!"

I did. It wasn't a bright night. You couldn't see moon or stars. But the sky was bright, all right. "Fire!" I said to Matty. "The whole city is burning!"

"What'll we do? Where will we go?" Matty ran on. "We don't know where the blaze is. We could be going straight for it. We don't know where we are or where we're going. The map is back in the hotel!"

"Cool it, Matty," I said. "This isn't like you, pal. Get a grip on yourself!" I hope I sounded in control, but to tell you the truth, I was hanging on the edge of panic myself. Maybe Matty getting shook up calmed me down. Matty fell silent for a second.

"You're right, Richie," he said in a soft voice. "I guess it was the ground moving that did it."

"Tell me about it," I said. "I nearly had to send my laundry out when it let go."

I looked up at the sky. "There must be more than one big fire," I said. "Look over that way." I pointed behind us. Matty glanced at where my finger led and grinned. He put a hand on my good shoulder.

"That's no fire, pal," he said. "It's the sun. It's daybreak. At least we'll see where we're going, even if we are lost."

Sure enough, the sun was coming up. We could now

make out figures of people wandering about the street. We weren't the only ones who'd got out of the buildings in time. On the sidewalk, looking like a tree in a meadow, a street clock was still standing. Its face was shattered and the lamp-post-like stalk it stood on was bent at a crazy angle. It read 5:12. That must have been when the quake hit.

We dusted ourselves off and began walking down the street. A fallen sign read Montgomery Street, but we couldn't tell where it had stood. I guess we should have tried to help the other people we saw wandering around, like we were. But what could we have done?

A woman, fully dressed, came toward us. I was about to ask her where Golden Gate Park was, but she spoke first.

"Have you seen my Jimmy?" she asked in a far-off voice.

"I haven't seen anyone but you so far, lady," I replied. "We're looking for Golden Gate Park. Do you know where that is?"

She looked straight through me. "Have you seen my Jimmy?" she repeated. Matty grabbed my arm.

"Let her alone, Richie," he said softly. "She's in shock."

"Shouldn't we try to help her?" I asked.

"Look around you, pal," Matty said. In the early morning light, we could see Montgomery Street was filled with people walking about aimlessly, just as much in shock as the woman. "What could we do? I'm no doctor, and that's what this lady needs." He looked down. "If it comes to that, I think we both need a doctor. Look at your feet, Richie."

He was right. Neither of us was wearing shoes. We'd been walking on broken glass and brick, and hadn't even noticed it. Matty's feet were bleeding; so were mine.

"I never felt a thing," I said.

"Me neither, till now," Matty said. "I guess we were both in shock. Just like her.... Where'd she go?"

The woman had walked off and was now talking to a disheveled man further down the street. Probably asking about her Jimmy. Now that I'd seen the shape my feet were in, I began to feel the pain.

"I think we better get some shoes to wear," I said.

"Sure thing," Matty said quickly, "soon as the stores open and we get some money to pay for them. Get real. I got an idea, though. We got our overcoats. Let's tear up the bathrobes and make foot coverings out of them."

"And be naked under our coats?"

"This is no time to get fussy, pal. Would you rather be dressed drafty or have cut-up feet?"

"I guess you're right," I said, glancing around before I shed my coat and took off my robe. I thought to myself that it was lucky we'd slept in those robes.

Using the belts to the robes to keep the terry cloth on our feet, we soon had some funny-looking cotton shoes. Like those pictures you see in history books of the troops at Valley Forge. Then off we marched, two naked guys in overcoats with fuzzy feet.

"Where are we going, fearless leader?" I asked.

"Well, the big fire seems to be that way," Matty said. "Judging by the sun, it's south and east of us. We don't want to go that way, so we should head northwest. Opposite from the flames."

It was getting quite light out now. We were able to see what was left of San Francisco plainly. Some terrible damage had been done. I guess that living in an age where you can see instant disasters on TV during the six o'clock news, the average kid of my time wouldn't have thought much of it. Buildings that still stood were gutted, and scores of small fires were springing up in the ruins.

We came to the intersection of Montgomery and California, and the streets were filled with people. They were all in the same sort of daze as the woman who was looking for her Jimmy. A man came toward us. He was dressed in a nightshirt and a derby hat, and had a violin case under his arm.

"Please, mister," I said, "which way is Golden Gate Park?"

"No Eenglish..." the man said with a sad smile. "No Eenglish." He walked on. As we walked along California Street, we saw more fellow victims of the quake. Some of them were still in their homes, looking down on the street, although the fronts of their houses were gone. I saw one man standing before a mirror in what must have once been his bathroom. He was shaving in the early morning light!

We walked two more blocks along California Street until we heard a commotion coming from behind us. We turned and saw a whole detachment of mounted soldiers. "Where did *they* come from?" I asked aloud. They were dressed perfectly, and their equipment glittered in the sun. The soldiers on horseback drew abreast of us, and I gave a start.

The horses had wrappings on their feet, just like Matty and I did. I realized why. If they struck sparks with their iron shoes, any escaping gas could explode. I ran up to the soldier riding in front of the group.

"Excuse me," I called out. "We're lost. Can you direct us to Golden Gate Park?"

The soldier held up his hand and gave a cry I couldn't get, but the whole column stopped behind him. I guess he said *whoa,* or whatever you say to stop cavalry. I wouldn't know; I'm no John Wayne fan.

"Are you two able to work?" he demanded.

"I guess so," I said. "Our feet are a bit cut up. We don't have shoes."

"That's not all you don't have," the soldier said with the hint of a smile. "Close your coat, man. There are women and children walking around here."

I glanced down and my face turned bright red. I hadn't thought to button my coat all the way down. It was a long winter coat, and it interfered with walking when buttoned tight. But being naked under it, I was on display for the world. I quickly closed it up.

"That's better," the soldier said. "Now, if you are un-wounded, you can work. There are people in need of help. I can't spare more than a corporal to go with you. You'll round up any able men you meet..."

He suddenly broke off speaking and cried out, "Good grief, your feet! Can't you feel them?"

Matty and I both looked down. The bottoms of our improvised terrycloth shoes were soaked in blood! I picked up one foot while standing on another. It looked terrible. Matty's weren't any better.

"They hurt a bit," I told the soldier.

"You're in no shape to be walking," the soldier said. "Go down to the end of this street. There's a cavalry trooper there with a cart. He's taking the injured to a field hospital we've set up. Tell him Lieutenant Carson sent you. If you can walk that far, he'll carry you to the doctor."

I didn't get a chance to reply. The soldier hollered to the troopers again, and they were off, with the horses at a slow walk. The horses' hooves made a muffled sound as they went, like a ghost troop of cavalry, plodding off to a funeral.

Matty and I walked down to where the soldier had told us, and found a number of sick or injured people in a big horse-drawn wagon. The sign on it read: *C & J Lehmann Wholesale Grocers.* The soldier in charge took one look at us and said, "Get in. We're just leaving for the field hospital." He didn't ask who sent us. I guess our feet were worse than we'd thought. Funny, they didn't feel that bad. Maybe we were still in shock. Looking down, I had to admit they looked terrible. At least the disaster had done one thing: erased the racial lines. We didn't have to say anything about Matty being black. A hurt man is a hurt man.

Just as I was getting into the wagon, I asked the soldier, "Where is this field hospital?"

"Not far, if you can fight the pain, kid," the trooper replied. "Just a few minutes away, in Golden Gate Park."

13

The Golden Gate

"How do you feel?" I asked Matty, once we were on our way.

"Funniest thing," he replied. "They don't hurt much at all. But my fuzzy shoes are soaked in blood. Yours, too. Shouldn't we feel weak from losing this much blood?"

"I don't know," I admitted. "I've never bled this much before."

"I guess the doctor will know," Matty said. "I'm a little worried, though. If these cuts get infected, we're in deep trouble. They don't have any antibiotics in 1906."

I looked around us at the people in the wagon. We seemed to be the only ones conscious. Mostly, the others were women and kids. But none of the kids were crying. Everyone was silent and sort of stunned. In about fifteen minutes' time, the wagon came to a groaning halt, and soldiers with stretchers came to the back end.

"It's all right," I said to the first one, "we can walk." The soldier looked at our feet. "You sure?"

"Yeah," I said. "Where's the doctor?"

"Hospital tent's just to your right, about a hundred yards. You can't miss it."

Matty and I limped to the tent and took our places in a line of about a dozen people to see the doctors. Soon I was seated on a stool, and a man in a white coat, spattered with blood, was unwrapping the terry cloth from my feet. He took one look at the right foot and swore long and loud.

"You don't need anything more than antiseptic," he said disgustedly. He grabbed at a bottle of something and dabbed at my foot. Then I did feel pain. It hurt like blazes.

"Ow!" I hollered.

"Oh, shut your mouth," the doctor said nastily. "All you have is scratches. Don't even need sutures."

"Then where did all the blood come from?" I asked.

The doctor picked up the discarded terry cloth and examined it. "Did you walk through any water?" he asked.

"I guess so. There were broken water mains and puddles all over."

"That's the answer, boy," the doctor said. "It's not blood. It's just brick dust from the debris, mixed with water. Your feet are cut, all right, but nothing serious." He looked at Matty behind me. "You too?" he asked.

Matty peeled off his cloth bindings from his feet and checked. "Yeah. Me too."

The doctor quickly applied more burning antiseptic to our feet, then hustled us out of the tent. "I have seriously injured people to treat," he grumbled after us as we left. Barefooted, we made our way toward some other tents, where people were milling about. We were halfway there when I realized I hadn't had the doc look at my shoulder.

To make it worse, I now felt a warm feeling on my right thigh. Was I bleeding? I looked around me. I'd have to hitch up my coat to check it out, and I was mother naked underneath. "Just a sec, Matty," I said. "I think I cut my leg."

Matty shielded me, and I lifted up the coat. My thigh was unmarked. I let the coat drop and felt the warmth again. I suddenly knew what it was. I reached into my coat pocket and nearly burned my hand. It was the key to the future gate, and it was getting hot! I began to laugh aloud.

"Are you okay, Richie?" Matty asked with concern.

"Me?" I said, almost dancing up and down. "Me? I'm great! Never better! I'm happy as a clam. I'm happy as a dozen clams!"

Just as Matty was about to think I'd gone batty, I pulled the key from my pocket. It was quite hot, and I tossed it at him. He fielded it expertly and then began to toss it back and forth from hand to hand like a hot potato. He began to laugh, too.

"We found it!" he cried happily. "We found it! It's right around here somewhere!"

We started looking right away. The newspaper item we'd read so long ago, in Houdini's office, had said the strange Spaniard had run behind "an outcropping of rock." Matty spotted it first. It wasn't too hard to do. There was a big chunk of rock, rearing up from the grass, with a long sheet of canvas on poles forming a screen in front of it.

"That's it. It's gotta be it," Matty said. "Is the key still hot?"

"Like a pistol," I said, and we both began running toward the canvas screen. We almost ran behind it immediately until we saw the crudely painted sign. *Women's Toilet.*

It made sense that they'd put the ladies' toilet there. It was the only place in the open field that was sheltered. Dig a trench in front of the rock, put a canvas screen around it, and *voilà!*, as Manfred would say, a private privy.

"How do we get inside?" I asked Matty. "Get ourselves up in drag?"

"Very funny," he replied. "Let me think."

We watched as women filed in and out for the next fifteen minutes. It was busy as a subway at rush hour. It must have been the only sanitary convenience for all the women who'd come here.

"We'll have to wait until nobody's using it," Matty said.

"When will that be?" I said. "It looks to me like there's more people arriving here every minute." I'd checked out the park, and it seemed it was being used to shelter all the homeless people from the quake. That was going to be one busy john.

"They have to sleep sometime," Matty said. "We'll wait until after dark."

It was maddening. Here was the gate we'd hoped to find, our way home—and it was on the site of a ladies' crapper! The hours seemed to drag until sunset. We wandered over to where some soup pots had been set up and got ourselves some watery chicken soup. Then it was back to the ladies' room for our vigil.

We'd just got back there and sat down when a soldier came up to us. He didn't look friendly, and he had his hand on a pistol holster at his side.

"I been watching you two," he said without a word of preamble. "You seem awful interested in the women's toilet...*too* interested. Stand up."

We got to our feet, and in doing so, the solider saw that we had nothing on under our coats. "Aha!" he hollered.

"I thought so! A couple of sex fiends! You two come with me." He took out his pistol for emphasis. I looked at Matty and he at me. We shrugged and put our hands up.

"Don't do that!" the soldier commanded. "It makes your coats open up. Ain't it bad enough you running around naked?"

"We lost our clothes in the quake," I protested.

"Sure, you did," the soldier said. "Come with me."

In ten minutes' time, we were inside a tent facing an officer, listening to the soldier report on us perverts. A few minutes later, we were in leg irons and handcuffs, inside a stockade with a bunch of looters and criminals.

We huddled together in a corner of the open-air enclosure, keeping well away from the others. The only thing that kept me from despairing was that they hadn't taken the key. We'd emptied our pockets, and finding we had no weapons, the officer allowed me to keep it. I'd said it was the key to my house. I don't think he believed me, but as long as it wasn't a weapon, he didn't care.

Night fell, and with it came a rotten pea-soup fog that chilled the bones. Pretty soon, you couldn't see a thing more than five feet away. I pulled my coat lapels closer around my bare chest, and my heart leaped as I felt something. I'd almost forgotten about it. I still had my set of lock-picking tools hidden in my overcoat lapel!

I quickly told Matty, and in a few seconds, we had opened the simple handcuff and leg-iron locks. We were free! Well, almost. There was still the barbed-wire enclosure to deal with. It was padlocked, and an armed guard walked back and forth in front of it, then made a tour around the whole setup. We edged closer to the front of the stockade, getting roundly cursed out by the sleeping looters we disturbed, then checked out the lock.

"Piece of cake," Matty announced. "I can get it open easy. Watch for the guard. We'll wait until he makes his circle."

The guard passed by, then disappeared into the thick fog. I'd heard of San Francisco fogs, but this one was ridiculous. Happily, the kerosene lantern that hung on the stockade gate cast enough light for Matty to see the lock. It sounded like a squeaky door when it opened, but it must have been my nerves. Matty swung the gate open, and we slipped out and began to run. From behind us, a voice called out "Halt!" and I heard a bang and something whistled past my ear!

We ran in the fog full tilt toward where we remembered the rock to be. I don't know how, but we found it. There was a lantern outside to guide late-night users of the privy, and we ran inside.

"What luck!" Matty whispered. "It's empty."

I took out the key, and it was glowing with an eerie blue light. We moved closer to the rock, stepping over a number of wooden buckets. Suddenly, the gloom of the privy was pierced by a bright, answering blue light that played about a whole section of the rock.

"Here we go," I said to Matty. We stepped toward the light, two paces. Then we turned, as though to walk away. Just as we were about to take the next steps that would have put us through the gate, a lady came into the privy. She took one look at us and opened her mouth to scream.

We never heard the scream. We took another step, and everything disappeared! A bright white light shone all around us. We seemed to be in a featureless, seamless white room. I didn't see a light source anyplace. Then a whole section of wall swung open, and into the room walked a huge man, clad in a white coverall kind of suit, with a hood that covered his hair and sort of formed a helmet.

"Congratulations, boys," he said. "Welcome to the future gate!"

I think it was then that I passed out.

14

The End of the Beginning

I woke up in a panic. I reached around me and grabbed only air. In some way I couldn't understand, I was suspended in midair! It took me a few seconds to figure out that I wasn't going to fall. In fact, I discovered that I couldn't fall, even when I tried. I looked around me and saw Matty, hanging in midair, the same way. He seemed to be unconscious until I heard him snoring lightly.

We were in the same white room, but now the color had changed to a restful darkish blue, and the light was quite subdued. As I sat up on thin air, the room began to brighten, and Matty stirred. He opened his eyes, rolled over, and saw me.

"Hiya, Richie," he said with a smile. "How do you feel?"

"Okay, I guess. But this is making me nervous...this floating."

"Nothing to it," Matty said. "It's just a bed, that's all. Works on some kind of force field. It's great when you think about it. No lumps in the mattress. And if we had 'em in 1976, it'd be a blessing for burn patients. If you want to get down, just *think* down."

Feeling somewhat silly, I thought to myself, *I want to stand up on the floor*. Slowly and gently, I began to settle at the foot end, while the rest of my body tilted until I was vertical. I felt the weight return to my feet, and there was no pain. I stood on one foot and checked the sole of the other. There were only fine-line scars there. I turned and saw Matty assuming a standing pose. He was wearing some sort of nightshirt made of clingy stuff. He was barefoot. I looked down and saw I was wearing the same kind of outfit.

"How long have I been out?" I asked.

"Not long. A couple of days."

"Did I hit my head when I passed out?"

"No, but you were under sedation until you healed. I was, too, but for less time than you. Did you notice your feet were all better?"

"Yeah, I did."

"They took care of that right away for me. They put you under because of your shoulder. You had a cracked collarbone, Richie."

"I never felt a thing."

"You were still in shock. The doctor says we both were."

"Matty, am I dreaming all this? Did that soldier really hit me with that shot? Tell me I'm not dead!"

"Easy, Richie," Matty soothed. "No, you're not dead and you're not dreaming either. But the gatekeeper will explain."

"But wait!" I cried out in panic. "You say we've been here for days. Doesn't that mean we're stuck here...wherever we are? Same as we were in the past?"

"Not at all," said a voice from behind me. I spun around to see the tall man I'd seen just before I passed out. He'd entered the white room through a section that swung open, like a door.

"But who?...What?..."

"Please," said the tall man, raising a hand, "I will explain it all to you. First, I am Julian, the gatekeeper of the future gate. No, you are not stranded in the future. You are inside the future gate itself. Time does not exist within the gate. But we need not remain in this medical cubicle."

He went to the wall and put his hand on a section of it. It swiveled open, like the "door" he'd entered from. He reached inside the open space and took out two white suits like the one he was wearing. "Put these on, and come with me," he said.

The suits were like bunny sleepers that kids wear. They had feet in them, as well as a hoodlike cowl that covered my hair. I felt like if the suit had ears and a tail, I could munch a carrot and ask Julian, "What's up, doc?"

Julian showed us how to close the suits once we got them on. You just pressed against a seam in the front, and it closed without a trace, right up to the neck. "Slick," I said to Julian, "but what happens when you have to go to the john? Do you have to take it off?"

Julian laughed. "The seam will open partially, Richard," he said. "From behind as well. Do you ask from need or curiosity?"

"Just curious."

"Very well, then. Come with me."

He led us through the still open "door," and we followed him down a long, bright corridor as featureless as the room we'd been in. Abruptly, we were in a vast, grass-covered meadow. Giant flowers of a type I'd never seen grew all around. But there were no trees. The highest structure I could see was miles away. It was a huge dome, wrecked and falling down. Nearby, there was a big rounded pile of stone that looked vaguely familiar.

"Where are we?" I asked.

"The question is *when* are we, Richard," Julian replied. "You are at exactly the spot from which you departed in 1906. Golden Gate Park. Except the year is, by your computation, 5406." He waved a hand at the domelike structure. "What you see there are the remains of the city of San Francisco. It was destroyed by nuclear war, many years ago."

"In my time? In the 1970s?"

"No, Richard. Hundreds of years later. But that makes it no less a tragedy."

"But now we're in the future. We're outside the gate," Matty said. "Won't we be stuck here if we stay too long?"

"We won't be here that long," Julian replied. He reached down and touched a part of his suit near the waist. Suddenly, a section of the rock outcropping began to glow. A...well, I guess you could call it a bubble of light detached itself and floated toward us. It was about twenty feet in diameter. I looked askance at Julian.

"It's a means of transportation, Richard," Julian said, as though he'd read my mind. "It will transport you almost instantaneously to the gate to the past, in Branford. You'll enter that gate, and it will bring you backward to your own time. But before you leave, there are a few things you should know. You two are the most important guests I have ever welcomed to my gate."

"Us? We're just a couple of musicians, Julian."

"Forgive me, Richard. You live in one small section of

time. I am aware of all that was and, up to a point, what will be. You and Matthew are very important for what you will one day become."

"I don't know if I want to know," Matty said.

"This is different. You will know, because in a sense, you already know. Or you will shortly. History says that you will."

"You mean to say we'll be in history books someday?" I asked.

"Indeed you will, Richard. You are part of history as the man who first discovered the time warp. Up until your time, it had been theorized, but never demonstrated. It remained for you and Matthew to do that. Prior to your round trip through time, people *did* fall through gates and become marooned. That cannot be changed: the Leonardo da Vincis, the Nostradamuses...the futurists and prophets. All accidental time travelers, stranded in the past. Because of you and Matthew, Richard Gilroy, the gatekeepers came into existence. In a sense, you are my creator, though I was designed many years after your death. However, death is a misleading term, in your case."

"*Designed?*" I asked. "What do you mean?"

"You are asking if I am truly a living being," Julian said. "No, I am not, physically. I am what you'd call in your time a robot. Though in the past, there was a real, living Julian. I am a reproduction of him, as the gatekeeper you met, Abner Pew, is a reproduction of a man who once was quite real. He fell into the gate to the past, mortally wounded. He was healed and lived a long, happy life. For a time, he was a gatekeeper, until technology devised machines such as me...us."

"But how did anyone know Pew would fall into time?"

Matty asked. "And how come someone was waiting to heal him?"

"Simple," Julian said with a smile. "Richard told us."

"No, I didn't!" I protested.

"Ah, but you *will*."

"I don't understand any of this," I said. Then I looked at Julian and said, "But I suppose I will?" He nodded and smiled again. Then he explained fully. I listened with my head spinning like a revolving door.

Finally, Julian said, "Now, it is time for you to go, boys. I don't have to wish you well, in your conversational convention. I know precisely how you will do. You have just to step inside the bubble, as you call it. It will take you immediately to Branford, and the gate to the past. The grave marker of Abner Pew is long gone, but you will see the portal. In this time period, there is no need to guard it."

"I wanted to ask about that," Matty said. "If you're a robot, and I haven't seen any people, where is everyone?"

Julian smiled and pointed skyward. "Man has left this planet by your year 5406. He has gone to the stars and other planets. Earth is largely one huge archeological dig. Now farewell!"

He turned and walked toward the big pile of rock, a flickering haze played about his figure, and then he was gone. Just like blowing out a candle. Matty and I looked at each other and stepped into the bubble.

"Do you think it'll take long?" Matty said.

"I don't think so. Look," I said. In front of us, before we had even noticed it was a field of flowers. But we were no longer in Golden Gate Park. The air felt different, and the land was shaped differently, too. The bubble vanished from around us. Directly in front of us stood an arch about seven feet high and five feet wide. It was made of some shiny metal.

"Do we do the same drill?" Matty asked.

"How should I know?" I replied. "I've never been here before."

"But Julian said you *will* be."

"Don't start that again," I said, and stepped toward the gleaming arch. Matty walked with me. We took the necessary steps, turned, and walked away. Into total darkness!

I felt the ground under my feet. It was irregular and semisoft. A breeze played across my face. "Matty?" I whispered, not knowing why I didn't speak louder.

"Right here, pal. Where are we?"

Just then, the moon broke through some ragged clouds above us. We were in the Branford Cemetery, facing the tombstone of Abner Pew! Then we went nuts, laughing, jumping up and down, and punching each other on the arm, slapping each other on the back. We'd done it. We'd gotten home! I called out in the dark for Abner Pew, but there was no answer. No matter. We knew we'd see him again. At least I would. Julian had told me.

Finally, we walked to the cemetery gate. When we saw Matty's Chevy, right where we'd left it, I could have kissed its tires. The only thing that proved it wasn't all a dream was the strange bunny suits we still wore. The 1976 clothes we'd left in the back of the Chevy were still there. We'd taken them off when we'd changed to 1940s stuff. It seemed so long ago. Well, it was. We stripped out of the spaceman stuff and put on jeans, shirts, and sneakers. Julian had been right. It was as though we'd never left.

Matty dropped me off at my house and we promised to

meet next day, at the Burger King. I slipped inside the house. Mom was passed out in front of the TV. A half-drunk tumbler of booze and diet cola was on the table in front of her. I turned off the TV, kissed her unfeeling face, and went to my room. Then I took a long shower and went to bed.

In the darkness, I stared at the ceiling and thought of what Julian had told Matty and me. It was hard to swallow, but in my heart, I knew it would all come to pass.

I would go to Nassau Community College in the fall, after taking makeup courses this summer. I would study history. I'd graduate with full honors and go on scholarship to Columbia University. After becoming the greatest historical scholar ever, thanks to my ability to do on-the-spot research, I would reveal how I'd done it: the time warp. But that wouldn't be until 1995.

I also knew that during one of my trips into the past, I'd be meeting Colonel Smith, father of Sister Amelia and founder of the Guiding Light Rescue Mission. I wondered what kind of man he'd be. And I wondered where I'd be getting the money to give him, so he could start up the Guiding Light.

Matty wouldn't go with me anymore in my time travels. He was going to be too busy. After all, hadn't Julian told us what would be? At age fifty-eight, and after a long career in Congress and the Senate as a prominent civil rights leader, Matty Owen would be sworn in as the forty-fourth president of the United States.

And why not? If anybody I know could talk himself into the White House, it would be Matty.

Bibliography

Cannell, J.C. *The Secrets of Houdini*. London: Hutchinson & Co., 1932.

Gresham, William Lindsay. *Houdini, The Man Who Walked Through Walls*. New York: Holt, Rinehart, & Winston, 1959.

Henning, Doug, and Reynolds, Charles. *Houdini, His Legend and His Magic*. New York: Times Books, 1977.

Laurie, Joe, Jr. *Vaudeville*. New York: Henry Holt & Co., 1953.

Samuels, Charles and Louise. *Once Upon a Stage, The Merry World of Vaudeville*. New York: Dodd, Mead & Co., 1974.

Spitzer, Marian. *The Palace*. New York: Atheneum Publishers, 1969.

Toll, Robert C. *On With the Show! The First Century of American Show Business*. London: Oxford University Press, 1976.

I also drew upon back issues of *Variety* and some of the newspapers I mention in the book. Finally, there were the author's personal recollections of the brief vaudeville revival that took place in New York City during World War II, when shortages of movie film stock prompted a return to the boards of such as Helen Kane, Smith and Dale, Joe Howard, Sr., Pat Rooney, and the Great Hardeen, still escaping from milk cans at age sixty-plus.